The *Final* Recollections of Charles Dickens

Books by Thomas Hauser

General Nonfiction

Missing

The Trial of Patrolman Thomas Shea

For Our Children
(with Frank Macchiarola)

The Family Legal Companion

Final Warning: The Legacy of Chernobyl
(with Dr. Robert Gale)

Arnold Palmer: A Personal Journey

Confronting America's Moral Crisis
(with Frank Macchiarola)

Healing: A Journal of Tolerance and Understanding

With This Ring
(with Frank Macchiarola)

A God to Hope For

Thomas Hauser on Sports

Reflections

Fiction

Ashworth & Palmer

Agatha's Friends

The Beethoven Conspiracy

Hanneman's War

The Fantasy

Dear Hannah

The Hawthorne Group

Mark Twain Remembers

Finding the Princess

Waiting for Carver Boyd

The Final Recollections of Charles Dickens

A NOVEL

The Final Recollections of Charles Dickens

Thomas Hauser

COUNTERPOINT | BERKELEY, CALIFORNIA

Library of Congress Cataloging-in-Publication is available.

ISBN 978-1-61902-586-8

Cover design by Ann Weinstock

Interior design by Neuwirth & Associates

COUNTERPOINT
2560 Ninth Street, Suite 318
Berkeley, CA 94710
www.counterpointpress.com

To my muse

Author's Note

This is a work of fiction. Throughout the manuscript, I have comingled Charles Dickens's words with my own. Prior to writing, I had the pleasure of reading all of Dickens's books and collected articles in addition to studying his times. I invite the reader to suspend disbelief and enjoy.

Thomas Hauser
New York, NY

The Final Recollections of Charles Dickens

Book 1

CHAPTER 1

I am heavy company for myself some times, weary in spirit and weary in flesh. My skin has gone from smooth to wrinkled, my hair from brown to gray. There is a weakness on my left side, and I am insecure in my gait. One foot or the other is always lame. The numbness in my hands comes and goes, as does the fluttering of my heart.

It is the year of Our Lord one thousand eight hundred and seventy. I am in my fifty-ninth year and fear that I am ready for the final bed.

I am Dickens. I have been acclaimed as the most important literary figure of my time. My books have enjoyed immense popularity and are welcome in every home. People of all classes take me by the hand and thank me for the pleasure that my writing has given them. I have been celebrated and accorded recognition seldom given to any man until his tomb becomes his throne.

Common men and women see themselves in my writing. My creations have been objected to on the high moral ground that some of the characters of my mind— thieves, embezzlers, prostitutes—have been chosen from the most criminal and degraded of London's population. I take no heed of those who condemn me for that reason. Lessons of the purest good may be drawn from the vilest evil. The dregs of life can serve the purpose of a moral just as well as the cream. Reminders of the truth that lie festering in squalid streets are as instructive as the flaunting of morality in Saint James.

In moments of candor, I acknowledge that I have shortcomings. I am impatient. I have a tendency toward self-pity. I have been called selfish, self-righteous, and vain. I am all of those things.

Yet no man ever worked more passionately or gave more of himself to his craft than I have given to my writing.

Before my time, literature as a profession had no distinct status in England. I please myself with thinking that my success has opened the way for others and that I will leave the position of literary men better and more independent than I found it.

Now as I travel the circle of my life near to its completion, I remember a time when my faults were not yet confirmed, when I was young and more idealistic than I am today. When my step was lighter and my hair not so gray.

I write now of that time. For many of my days, I have been the most public of men. Yet I have kept the most important chapter of my life private and hidden from view.

I write now with the wisdom of a life fully lived and with the honesty of one who senses that the grave is near.

I write so that, when I pass from this world, the events and people that I am about to describe shall be remembered forever.

❦

I was born in Portsea on 7 February 1812. England had yet to develop a social conscience. The rich lived in blessed isolation from the poor. A common language was their only bond.

My paternal grandparents were of the servant class. In 1805 their son, John Dickens, became a clerk in the Navy pay office. Four years later he married Elizabeth Barrow, whose father had been a lieutenant in the Navy. I was the second of eight children and first son born to John and Elizabeth Dickens.

My father was a genial man who spent beyond his means and was often in debt. He lived with a sense of entitlement unjustified by any measure. We changed residences frequently when I was a child to evade his creditors.

I was a shy boy and not at all robust, quickly run over in a crowd.

My early education and passion for books were gifts from my mother. She initiated me in the mysteries of the alphabet and taught me to read when I was young. As a child, I read in my bed every night until it grew too dark to see the letters. Nothing ordained that I should become a writer. It was simply in me.

When I was ten years old, reforms in the Admiralty necessitated that my father move the family to London.

The city has changed since then. It was far less ordered and secure when I was young than it is now. Worse, the science of sanitation was largely unknown. A deadly waterway that had once been a fine fresh river flowed through the heart of the city. Open sewers ran through the streets, their contents coming to rest in blockages or larger pools of vile-smelling filth. Many sewers poured directly into the Thames, from which the people of London took their water.

A cycle of disease pervaded the slums and emanated outward. The poor had yet to be taught to wash their bodies and clean their clothes. Lice were an accepted part of grooming. People lived so unwholesomely that rain water put into their crowded rooms on Saturday night would be corrupt on Sunday morning. Cholera, smallpox, scarlet fever, and typhus were common. Almost half of the deaths in London were of children under the age of ten.

Our home in London was a small tenement with a little back-garden. Yet even then, my father continued to live beyond his means, and debt became an even more pressing problem. The books I had treasured as a child were sold for a pittance to keep creditors at bay. The appearance at our door of merchants and other trades-people demanding payment was constant in our lives.

My father borrowed two hundred pounds more, defaulted on that debt too, and failed to make required tax payments. In February 1824, he was arrested for defaulting on a forty-pound obligation owed to a local baker and was sent to Marshalsea prison.

Under the law of that time, my father could be released from prison once there was an adjudication that our family possessions had a value of not more than twenty pounds. Meanwhile, as was the custom of those days, my mother and younger siblings went to live with him at Marshalsea.

It was an evil hour for me. A relative on my mother's side of the family who was familiar with our plight proposed that I go to work in a blacking warehouse, where black polish for boots was made from tallow, wax, soda ash, and oil and was put into pots for sale. The offer at a salary of six shillings a week was quickly accepted by my parents.

On a Monday morning, two days after my twelfth birthday, I went to the warehouse to begin my new life. It is a source of wonder to me that I was so easily cast into the cold hard world at such a young age by my mother and father.

The warehouse was a rotting large building that abutted the Thames. When I think of it now, the large gray rats swarming in the cellar and the dirt and decay of the place rise up before me as if I were there again.

Six days a week for ten hours each day, I sat at a table on the first floor. My work was to cover the pots filled with blacking, first with a piece of oil-paper and then with a piece of blue paper, then to tie them round with a string, and finally to clip the paper close and neat until it looked as smart as a pot of ointment from an apothecary's shop. When a certain number of pots had attained this perfection, I was to paste on each a printed label and then go on again with more pots.

As for lodging, I was handed over to an old lady who took children in to board. Two other boys and I slept in the same room. I provided for my own breakfast of a penny loaf and a penny-worth of milk each morning. I kept another small loaf and cheese on a particular shelf in a particular cupboard to make my supper when I returned each night. I tried to make my money last the week by putting it in a drawer at the warehouse, wrapped into little parcels, each parcel containing the same amount and labeled with a different day of the week.

Some times, going to work in the morning, I could not resist the stale pastry put out at half-price on trays at the confectioners' doors. I would spend on pastry the money I should have kept for dinner and then go without dinner. When I had money enough, I would go to a coffee shop and have half a pint of coffee and a slice of bread and butter. When I had no money, I took a turn in Covent Garden market and stared at the pineapples.

I was both mother and father to myself. I received no advice, no encouragement, no consolation, no support from anyone. I kept my own counsel and did my work. I suffered in secret. I was miserably unhappy and considered my circumstances to be hopeless. My early dreams of growing up to be a learned distinguished man were crushed in my breast. My whole nature was penetrated with grief and humiliation and a feeling of vulnerability to the vagaries of chance. For all the care that was taken of me, I could easily have become a vagabond or robber. With a few more unfortunate twists, my fate would have been a never-ending downward spiral.

My father was released from Marshalsea after three months' imprisonment. At my mother's suggestion and with his consent, I remained at the blacking warehouse. Finally, after I had been there for more than a year, my father decreed that I should return to school. It was not a matter of his caring about my condition so much as it was that his pride was wounded by my servitude.

I do not write in anger of that time in my life, for I know how all things worked together to make me what I am. But I can never forget, and shall never fully forgive, that my mother favoured my being sent back to the blacking warehouse. After I was freed, I could not endure to go near it. For many years, I would cross over to the opposite side of the road when passing by so as to avoid the smell of the cement they put upon the blacking corks, which reminded me of what I once was.

At age thirteen, with the blacking warehouse behind me, I enrolled in school at Wellington House Academy. But my father's financial condition remained precarious, and we moved frequently from one residence to another. Soon after my fifteenth birthday, he was unable to pay the cost of my lessons, and my formal schooling came to an end.

In 1827, I accepted a position as a writing clerk in the legal offices of Ellis and Blackmore. For the most part, I copied documents by hand and carried them to and from other attorneys' offices and various courts. It was tedious work for which I was paid ten shillings, six pence a week.

While at Ellis and Blackmore, I began learning shorthand with an eye toward becoming a stenographer. It was a difficult art. My waking hours, and also my sleep, were troubled by the changes in dots, which in one position meant one thing and in another position meant something entirely different. I was tormented by the vagaries played by circles and the unaccountable consequences that resulted from marks like a fly's leg in a wrong place. Once I had groped my way through these difficulties, there appeared a procession of new horrors called arbitrary characters, which insisted that a scrawl like the beginning of a cobweb meant one thing and a sky-rocket stood for something else having nothing to do with the sky or a rocket.

I tamed the savage shorthand beast and left Ellis and Blackmore after eighteen months to work as a stenographer at Doctors' Commons. The name of the court was derived from the degree held by those who practiced there: doctors of civil law. It was a place where marriage licenses were given to lovesick couples and divorces were granted to husbands and wives who had grown sick of each other. It was also where wills were registered and certain small legal matters were adjudicated by trial.

It was not a bad living for me, but it was not a particularly good one either. And my eye was on a more ambitious goal. In 1831, at age nineteen, I joined the staff of *The Mirror of Parliament*, a weekly publication that reported on proceedings in the House of Lords and House of Commons. My work consisted of attending legislative sessions and transcribing what was spoken.

It has been said that one must be a common scholar before becoming an uncommon one. In 1833, I took the first tentative step in that direction. I had previously applied for and received a reader's card for the library in the British Museum. Now I had a desire to put my own thoughts on paper rather than read and record the words of others.

I wrote a sketch of London life and submitted it anonymously to a little-known publication called the

Monthly Magazine. I was so unsure of myself that I dropped my work stealthily into a letter box outside a dark office one evening at twilight. A week later, "Dinner at Poplar Walk"—my writing—was published.

I purchased a copy of the magazine, walked to Westminster Hall, and went inside. I remained there for half an hour because my eyes were so dimmed with joy and pride that they could not bear the light of the street and were not fit to be seen.

A vision of what my life might become had opened wide before me.

More sketches followed. In August 1834, I published my first signed article in *the Monthly Magazine* using the pseudonym "Boz"—a pet name that had been bestowed upon one of my younger brothers. That same month, I took a job as a reporter for the *Morning Chronicle.* Unlike my work as a Parliamentary reporter, my new position offered a regular salary. That enabled me to move out of my parents' home and establish a residence of my own.

My responsibilities at the *Morning Chronicle* largely involved the transcription of speeches, debates, and talks given at political dinners and other political events. When Parliament was not in session, I did general reporting and wrote theatre reviews for the paper.

Theatre was a love of mine. I harboured ambitions as an actor and practiced even such things as walking in and out of a room and sitting down in a chair so as to impress others. I attended some form of theatre almost every night at that time in my life. But the sketches, which were my first attempts at true authorship, remained the focus of my writing. I am conscious of their bearing

marks of haste and inexperience. I was a young man,
and I sent them into the world with many imperfec-
tions. Nonetheless, I recorded London and its people
as I found them.

The *Morning Chronicle* published *Sketches by Boz* on a regular basis. Then, in January 1835, one of its owners,
George Hogarth, undertook to edit a new paper. Hogarth asked me to write sketches for *The Evening Chronicle*. I
agreed, and my salary was increased from five to seven
guineas a week.

Hogarth also invited me to his home in Chelsea,
where I was introduced to his eldest daughter, Catherine.

There had been little romance in my life up until
that time. I was slightly built and looked young for my
age. Carrying myself with perfectly erect posture, I was
able to appear a bit taller than I was. My features were
characterised more by animation and, I would hope,
intelligence than by beauty and grace. Later, my fame
became an aphrodisiac. Women wanted to be in my
presence. But I was largely ignored by the descendants
of Eve when I was young.

Catherine was amiable, sweet natured, and kind.
Also short, plump, and awkward in movement. It was
a time in my life when I wanted a family and to be the
master of my own home. I greatly admired her father,
and he saw me as a young man of promise. The relationship also offered me a passageway to a more secure
position in society.

There is an adage that advises, "A man should select
for his wife only such a woman as he would select for a
friend were she a man."

By that measure, I chose unwisely. In May 1835, I proposed marriage to Catherine, and she accepted without pause.

Better had she not. There is no disparity in marriage more troublesome than unsuitability of mind. Catherine had no interest in the world beyond her family and no experience with it either. She was of a social class above me but made a poor lion's mate.

At the time, I did not understand.

Meanwhile, I continued to write. *Sketches by Boz* grew more popular. In autumn of 1835, a publisher named John Marone offered me one hundred pounds for their copyright with the intention of publishing them with illustrations in two volumes the following year.

That brings my narrative to 27 January 1836, when George Hogarth invited me to dine with him at the Garrick Club. The club had been founded five years earlier for the purpose of bringing together patrons and practitioners of drama, so that actors and others of the theatre might meet on equal terms with men of education and wealth.

The day was clad in one of the least engaging of the three hundred and sixty-five dresses in the wardrobe of the year. It was raw, damp, and dismal. In the country, the rain would have developed a thousand fresh scents, and every drop would have had its bright association with some beautiful form of life. In the city, it had a foul stale smell and was a dirt-stained addition to the gutters.

We dined in a large room with richly paneled walls before retiring to the club library. A gentleman with a hook attached to his right wrist approached another man who was standing by the fireplace.

The man by the fireplace was in his mid-thirties with a sharp nose and prominent chin. He was elegantly dressed in a brown suit with a shirt of the finest linen, rich in pattern and scrupulously white. He seemed a bit haughty, as though requiring everyone who wished conversation to come to him. And come they did, each visitor enjoying an audience for so long as he politely allowed.

Think for a moment of a long chain woven around a man that has a hold upon his thoughts for the rest of life. A chain of iron or thorns or flowers or gold. That chain would not exist to bind him but for the formation of the first link on the first day.

For everything that followed in my life, this was that day.

As a writer of fiction, I have been privileged to come and go as I please, to enter through keyholes, to ride upon the wind, to overcome all obstacles of distance, time, and place. But the recitation contained in the following pages is truth in its most absolute form. Whatever contradictions and inconsistencies were within me, whatever might have been done differently and better, this is as I acted and as it all happened to me.

CHAPTER 2

The man standing by the fireplace in the library of the Garrick Club was not handsome. But he had the carriage of a handsome man and an aura about him that demanded attention. He stood with his arms folded for greater impressiveness of bearing. Everyone in the room was aware of his presence. I watched as he talked with those who ventured to his side and observed how readily they responded to him.

"That's Geoffrey Wingate," George Hogarth told me. "He's an ingenious man."

I knew of Wingate by reputation. Gentlemen on the street raised a forefinger to the brim of their hat as he passed by. He was a man of business who invested with great success on behalf of his clients, who were drawn from the ruling class. His money and the money he had made for them had caused him to be courted and admired.

"I met him at a dinner not long ago," Hogarth confided. "I think he will remember me. Would you like an
introduction?"

I thought that would be interesting, and Hogarth
clearly wanted to remake Wingate's acquaintance. So we
crossed the room to the fireplace.

Wingate acknowledged our approach. "Mr. Hogarth.
It is a pleasure to see you again."

His voice was deep and rich. It seemed incongruous
that a man of ordinary stature should have such a large
voice, almost intimidating in the manner of physical
bulk.

Hogarth introduced me as "the young man who is
betrothed to my lovely daughter, Catherine."

Wingate said that he was pleased to meet me, but
there was no overdoing of it. He was pleased to meet me
in a well-bred, mannered way. Then Hogarth added that
I was "better known as Boz," and Wingate's demeanor
changed.

"Very impressive," he noted. "You are such a young
man. You must tell me how your writing began."

I was brief in my recitation. Then, to my surprise,
Wingate handed me his card with the instruction, "We
must talk further soon."

"I know how precious your time is," I said deferentially.

"Nonsense."

"A sketch by Boz in *The Evening Chronicle* would interest
our readers," Hogarth offered. "And nicely done, it
could advance Mr. Wingate's business interests."

"Precisely," Wingate responded. "Mr. Dickens and I
must set up a time to talk. I conduct business from my

home. Would Monday next at two o'clock in the afternoon be convenient for you?"

I said that it was.

"I will see you then. For now, let me leave you with
the thought that every man should live as comfortably as
he can. My advice to you, sir, is, 'Be as rich as possible.
Be as rich as you honestly can.'"

Wingate lived in a large house on a genteel street near
Grosvenor Square. I arrived for my appointment a few
minutes before the appointed hour. A brass knocker
shaped like the head of a ferocious lion glared at me
from the front door. I wiped my boots and was admitted
by a servant.

The house was spacious and grandly furnished
with rich sofas, handsome mirrors, and high-backed
damask-covered chairs. A second servant led me
through several rooms and knocked on a closed
oak door. Wingate's voice sounded loud and clear,
instructing me to enter. I did, and he rose from his
desk to greet me.

The room was magnificently furnished with formi-
dable easy chairs, thick carpet, and cabinets inlaid with
precious wood. A window behind an imposing leather-
topped desk looked out on a plot of land cultivated as a
garden. It was not the best time of year for a garden, but
I could see that the space was beautifully kept. There
were clusters of bushes and trellises on which flowers
would bloom in the growing season.

A large oil painting facing the window depicted a naval engagement with two warships firing cannonry at each other while several more vessels were blowing up in the distance.

Wingate and I shook hands, and he gestured for me to sit opposite the desk. Then he took a seat. A thick green ledger with a red leather spine lay open before him.

"I took the liberty of making some inquiries about your past," Wingate said, beginning the conversation. "I am sure that, as a reporter, you will do the same of me if you have not already done so. Frankness is part of my character, so let me be direct and honest with you."

"I was not born in the front rank. I have no trophies of birth. It was not preordained that I should be a gentleman. Like you, I was forced by circumstances to make my own way in the world. I am what you aspire to be. If a man is born in possession of a silver spoon, it is not very difficult to keep the spoon polished. But if he is born in possession of a wooden ladle, the process of transmuting it to silver can be discouraging. I am thirty-six years old and a rich man now. Not so rich as some suppose, but wealthy. I have fought against the inequities of the world, and I have won."

"My business involves the combination of financial judgment and capital. Others supply the capital. I put in my ability and knowledge. I arrange investments, annuities, insurance, and other business ventures on the most favourable terms possible for my clients in exchange for a small commission. The dividends on most of the investments that I arrange begin immediately and are substantial. I am a bold speculator but not a reckless one. I know what to invest in and how to back out quietly at the right time as well as any man alive. There is strict integrity in all of my transactions. There must be absolute honour among men of business, or business cannot be successfully carried on."

Wingate reached for the ledger on his desk and took a sheaf of documents from one of the cabinets. Books, papers, statements, and calculations were soon spread out before me. The entries were written in his own hand in a neat and precise manner.

"Examine the affairs of my business for yourself so that you completely understand them," he told me. "Then, write what you will. And if you feel comfortable with the idea, I would welcome your participation."

"I have no money to invest."

"That is not what I had in mind," Wingate said with a benign smile. "In your work, you encounter many people. Most of them have no money to invest, but some do. For any new investors that you bring to the company, I would pay you a small commission. It would take little effort or time on your part."

"I would have to know more before committing myself to your cause."

"Study my business. Look into anything and everything as you choose. Pursue a situation with me, and it will make your fortune."

Wingate stood up and moved away from his desk, a sign that our meeting was over. He walked me to the door of his office . . . opened it . . . and I heard music.

"Amanda is playing," he told me. "Come, you must meet my wife."

He led me through the house to a room off the parlour. A woman sitting in a chair was running her fingers along the column strings of a Celtic harp. She was my age, possibly a year or two younger.

I had never seen a woman so beautiful before. I am quite certain of that. Even in my imagination, it would have been difficult to create such beauty. Her face was magnificent, every feature clearly defined. Her cheekbones were high, her nose perfectly formed, her complexion fair. I wondered what colour her eyes were when, at that moment, she turned to face me.

Hazel.

"Allow me to introduce my wife," Wingate said. "Mr. Dickens, this is Amanda. Amanda, this is Mr. Charles Dickens. He intends to write about my business."

Amanda Wingate rose and offered her hand. She was almost as tall as I was, exquisitely shaped with a full bust and slender waist. Her chestnut-coloured hair fell in waves below her shoulders. Nature had given her the carriage of a lady. There was majesty in her eye.

"I hope that I am not the cause of your ceasing to play such beautiful music," I offered.

"My goodness, no."

"Why did you not go on then?"

"I left off as I began, of my own fancy."

The light of the late-afternoon sun danced on the floor, filtering through the colours of a small stained-glass window.

First impressions last for a long time. This one would last forever.

No further words were spoken other than the pleasantries of parting.

Geoffrey Wingate walked me to the front door. "You may be perfectly certain of one thing," he said as I took my leave. "I am an honest man. Truth is a friend to those who are good."

＊

There was a great deal to do in the aftermath of my meeting with Wingate. Fourteen months earlier, my brother Frederick and I had moved into chambers at Furnival's Inn. We had three small rooms, none of which were big enough to swing a cat in. I had not wanted to swing a cat, so that was of no concern to me. But now, in preparation for my marriage to Catherine, I signed a lease on larger accommodations in the same dwelling.

On the eighth day of February, one day after my twenty-fourth birthday, *Sketches by Boz* was published in two volumes. Meanwhile, I had been approached by another publisher and asked to write a series of adventures about a gentlemen's sporting club with characters who come and go like the men and women we encounter in the real world. It was intended that the series, entitled *The Pickwick Papers*, be published in monthly serial numbers of twenty-four pages each, a form known to me only by recollection of a class of novels carried about the country by peddlers. I agreed to the undertaking because I was to be paid fourteen pounds, three shillings for each serial part.

I also decided that I should make further inquiry into Geoffrey Wingate's business before I wrote about him. In essence, he sold pieces of paper bearing a pledge to pay substantial sums in return. Then he invested his client's money in the stock of public companies;

commodities such as wine, silver, and coal; annuities; insurance; and other business ventures. My time in the courts had given me a rudimentary understanding of financial institutions. But I found it difficult to get a firm grasp on his business dealings.

I went first to the stock market. The trading of shares in public corporations had begun in London in the late seventeenth century with the need to finance two ocean voyages. The Muscovy Company had been seeking trade with China. The East India Company had its eye fixed on India. The owners of the companies required capital beyond private financing to undertake the voyages, so they sold shares to merchant investors in exchange for a portion of their profits. The idea spread as an innovative form of business. By the end of the seventeenth century, there were one hundred and fifty public stock companies in London. Shares were bought and sold in two coffee shops near Change Alley. Then Parliament enacted laws requiring that all sellers of stock be licensed. In the mid-eighteenth century, these sellers opened a club known as The Stock Exchange in a building on Sheeting's Alley. In 1801, the club was made subject to official regulation as the London Stock Exchange.

It followed as a natural consequence of things that, when I went to the stock exchange to inquire about Geoffrey Wingate, the man I wanted to see was not in his office, and no one knew where he was or when he would return. I went back for a second visit with similar success, only this time, I was criticised by a clerk for meddling in the affairs of the upper class.

A review of public records was similarly unenlightening. On the sixteenth of February, I visited the office of the clerk at Doctors' Commons in the hope that someone there could tell me something of value.

It was a reunion of sorts with old acquaintances. We talked about days gone by and my new life.

There was a young man I did not know, one of several whose job it was to keep the building clean. He stopped his sweeping and listened as I talked with the others.

"Geoffrey Wingate," he said in a manner that drew my attention.

"Yes?"

"He killed a man, you know."

There were utterances of surprise from around the room. Then silence.

"I did not know," I responded. "Tell me more."

"The story is not mine. It belongs to a friend."

"Can I speak with him?"

The request was met with a reluctant look.

"I will ask if that is possible."

On the next day and the day after, I returned to Doctors' Commons with increasing curiosity. The sweeper was nowhere to be found. When I arrived on the third day, he was standing outside the main entrance to the building.

"Tomorrow at eleven o'clock in the morning," he instructed. "Be here. My friend will find you. It would be best if you dressed with no sign of wealth so as not to attract attention of the wrong kind."

Well before the appointed hour on the following day, I was outside Doctors' Commons. My dress was shabby, which ran counter to my preferred appearance.

A clock in the tower of a nearby church struck eleven times. A man about my age moved to my side.

"Mr. Dickens?"

He was of average height, with long hair, intelligent eyes, and a nose that had been broken several times. His shoulders were broad. The coat he wore had once been a smart dress garment, but at that long-ago time it had adorned a smaller man. The soiled and faded sleeves were short on his arms. His trousers were patched in a manner that spoke of long service. His shoes were mended. He had the look of a labourer.

"My name is Christopher Spriggs. I have come to guide you and ensure your safe passage."

"I am told that Geoffrey Wingate killed a man."

"And worse."

"Come, now, what could be worse than killing a man?"

"I will show you."

Our journey began.

There are places that one who holds a certain station in life does not go. Christopher Spriggs took me to them. We walked through the civilised part of London and several miles beyond into a world where poverty, ignorance, and disease are as certain as death.

The streets were foul and narrow, the shops and houses wretched. The air was impregnated with filthy odours. The roughest and poorest of people thronged the streets. Hunger was everywhere. It oozed out of doors and stared down from smokeless chimneys. It was in the faces of children, sickened from want and cold, existing upon the smallest portion of the weakest food necessary to keep them alive.

Christopher Spriggs walked with a brisk, purposeful stride. There was little conversation between us. When he spoke, his voice was soft but clear. A dozen children dressed in rags surrounded us like a pack of feral dogs. Christopher raised his hand as if to strike, and they retreated. A deformed boy watched from nearby.

"It is a sad thing," Christopher said, "to see a crippled child apart from the others. When they are active and merry, he sits alone, watching the games that he cannot share in."

We continued past tottering housefronts, half-crushed chimneys, and windows guarded by rusty iron bars. Narrow alleys branched off onto passageways that were more remote and less frequented than those we travelled. Unemployed labourers and brazen women called out from the rutted dirt in front of homes that were one step removed from rubbish. Lofty church steeples rose proudly to mock it all.

Several hours after our journey began, we came to a particularly wretched hovel. Christopher motioned for me to go inside. I lowered my head at the door and entered.

The room had a flavour of rats sleeping close together in dark holes. Spiders had built webs in the angles of the ceiling and walls. Four rough beds made of tattered sacks lay on the floor. There was a low cinder fire in an unfixed rusty grate, a rickety wood chair, and an old stained table with several plates and cups on top. Heaps of rags and small bundles lay in corners of the room. Those were the only possessions I saw.

I could imagine no gaiety of heart in this home, only life on the lowest terms that could sustain it. Everything was black with age and dirt. Hell was breeding there.

An infant lay sleeping in an old egg crate. A woman, presumably the child's mother, sat beside her. She was in profile to me, plainly dressed with a look of beauty about her.

"This is the gentleman I spoke of," Christopher Spriggs told the woman. "He would like to know of Geoffrey Wingate."

There was no response.

"Mr. Dickens, this is my sister, Florence."

Florence Spriggs turned to face me. And I recoiled in horror.

CHAPTER 3

Florence Spriggs could trace her genealogy all the way back to her mother. She also knew that she had a brother, Christopher, who came into the world one year before she did. She had no knowledge of where she was born, only that the event occurred in 1812. The identity of her father was unknown.

Florence's earliest memory dated to the age of four on the night when her mother died. There was neither fire nor candle. She died in the dark. Florence and Christopher could not see her face, though they heard her gasping out their names.

After their mother's death, the children were taken in as an act of charity by a wealthy landowner. Frederick Clarke and his wife lived on a manor in Leicestershire. It was intended that Florence and Christopher would be servants at an older age.

Florence was taught to read. She was also taught that she was different from the master's children because she was an orphan and was from a lower class. They looked down on her and reminded her often of her status. In the little world in which children exist, there is nothing so finely perceived and felt as injustice. Through no fault of her own, there was a shadow on Florence's life. But she vowed that she would be industrious and kind, do good deeds, and be deserving of love.

As a child, Florence was pretty. Then she passed through the state of weeds common to girls of a certain age and burst into flower. By her thirteenth birthday, nature had painted her more beautifully than any artist's hand could render. Her long red hair hung free in ringlets. Her blue eyes sparkled like jewels. Putting her beauty into words was like trying to hold a ray of sunlight in one's hand. The master of the house rebuked a business partner for suggesting that Florence would be a desirable sexual pleasure when a bit older. He was already aware of the possibility and thinking of time and place himself.

The manor was fully staffed with a butler, housekeeper, valet, maids, cooks, coachman, groom, stable boy, footmen, and gardeners. A governess assisted the mistress where the rearing and education of the children was concerned. A nurse tended to the babies.

Florence was assigned chores as an aide to the governess. Christopher worked in the gardens. Together, they were friends with James Frost, who had come to the manor when Florence was nine. He was also an orphan and was one year older than she was.

James, Christopher, and Florence explored the mysteries of the world together.

"I caught a frog in the stream this morning," James told them one day. "It had two eyes."

"All frogs have two eyes," Florence said, laughing.

"Please, let me finish. The frog led me to further thought. All people and animals have two eyes. All birds and all bugs have two eyes. It is always two. Never one or three. Why do you think God made it that way?"

When it rained, Florence and James loved to watch the falling drops and smell the fresh scents. When the wind blew, they delighted in fancying what it said. They walked hand in hand in the sunshine through flowery meadows. The dew sparkled more brightly on the green leaves, the air rustled among them with sweeter music, and the sky looked more blue and bright when they were together. They loved each other with greater purity than can be found in the best love of a later time in life. They made no more provision for growing older than they did for growing younger.

On the day that changed Florence's life forever, she was walking with James in the meadow. It was scant weeks past her fourteenth birthday.

"I see no reason why I should be a servant girl forever," Florence told him. "I want to be a lady. And you should be a gentleman."

She glowed with the grace of young beauty. The sun and moon and stars were made to light her.

"If I was ever to be a lady, I would give you a blue coat the colour of the sky with diamond buttons, a large gold watch, a silver pipe, and a box of money."

James was young and handsome with a keen dark eye and a heart filled with every pure and true affection that a young woman could cherish.

"If you were a lady, all I would ask for is your heart."

He would forever remember that day in the meadow

and the flowers in Florence's hair. Forget-me-nots. As if forget-me-nots were needed for him to remember her.

She looked at him with eyes that were radiant and true. He returned her gaze with eyes that were honest and beaming with hope.

Her lips were ripe and made to be kissed.

So he kissed her.

That night, the master summoned Florence to his lair. The attractive little bud was flowering with the blush of womanhood. It was time to take her.

He offered her wine. She drank half a glass out of polite obligation, then stopped. She did not like the feel of the moment. He suggested that she drink more. She declined.

Then he took her forcefully for his pleasure.

Florence fought to preserve her honour, but resistance was futile. She cried out for help. No one came to save her. She remembered now hearing similar cries from other servant girls in the house at night and the haunted look in their eyes the following morning.

When it was done, she had lost what no one could give back to her. He had taken what could never be returned. She slept not at all that night. In the morning, the master's valet handed her a small silk purse with three gold sovereigns in it.

Florence now had a father. She was a daughter of shame. She stayed sick in her room all that day. Her hopes of growing up to be a lady lay crushed in her breast. When night fell, she packed up her few belongings and fled from her childhood home.

She told no one what had happened. She did not want

James or Christopher to know of her degradation. It was better to disappear than to have them know.

She walked for hours, then stopped to rest in a church. Not many people care to sleep in a church. I do not mean at sermon time, when it is often done. I speak of at night and alone. The angry wind has a dismal way of wandering round and round and moaning as it goes, of trying the windows and doors and seeking out crevices by which to enter. Once it has got in, it wails and howls and stalks through the aisles, glides round the pillars, soars up to the roof, flings itself despairingly upon the stones below, and passes, muttering, into the vaults. It has an awful voice, the wind in a church at midnight.

After three days' travel, Florence arrived in London. With her ever-diminishing three sovereigns, she bought the food necessary to survive. Half a loaf was better than crumbs. Crumbs were better than nothing. She joined the working poor, whose hands are hardened by toil. A decent woman spoke to her about needlework and lodging. She found a position as a seamstress for a dressmaker.

Florence's new home was a large whitewashed room behind a dress shop shared with eight other women. The stifled air and dim light were what one expects in such a situation. Each woman had a shelf on which to place her personal belongings. Large hooks fixed in the wall beneath the shelves served as the hanging place for mats and blankets. There was a fireplace and a long table at which the women sat on wooden benches for dinner.

Florence worked early and late. She strained her eyes until it was too dark to see the threads, then lit a candle and worked longer. It was cheerless, never-ending toil; not to live well, but to scrape together enough to live.

She hid her beauty as best she could. But in due course, the proprietor of the shop took notice of her shape and general appearance and decided that Florence would look appealing in a low dress with long sleeves made full in the skirts with four tucks in the bottom. And in just about anything else, for that matter.

It became part of her duties to exhibit the dresses for customers.

Men looked at her often when she ventured onto the streets, but she wanted no part of them. She had been ruined. Let the lips of no honest man touch hers ever again.

She thought often of James Frost and wished that he would have a good life. She truly loved him.

Time passed.

A woman named Hortense Webster came to the shop. She was forty years old and quite portly with an expanding stomach and ample bust. Her jewels bespoke her wealth.

Hortense talked with Florence in a friendly way. She asked about her circumstances and invited her to tea. Florence was flattered that so fine a lady took an interest in her.

All the while at tea, Hortense was studying Florence. The young woman's voice was sweet and musical. She spoke nicely. Her manner was timid, but she had self-possession and control over her emotions. Although made up in a plain way, she was beautiful with an aura of innocence about her.

The longer that Hortense studied Florence, the more she saw a fortune in her beauty.

"When there are two parties to a bargain," Hortense told Florence, "it is right that the interests of both sides be met."

Then Hortense Webster offered Florence a new life, one of ease and comfort. All that would be required of her, from time to time, would be to lay with a man.

The sale of women has been a part of every society from the beginning of history. It has been widely condemned as an affront to God, yet it has always flourished. Prostitution is older than any of the world's Holy Books. It is spoken of in the Bible and the written record of every culture.

Man is endowed by nature with passions that must be gratified. No blame can be attached to him who seeks a woman of pleasure to fulfill his needs. This is the rationale that has always been used to justify the conduct of the purchaser in the transaction. Men and women of all classes in every age have known the pleasures and degradation of prostitution. It has never been, and never will be, eradicated in any place or time.

Some women are drawn to prostitution by a love of sex and excitement, but they are few in number. For most, it is poverty that draws them in. They have lived in filth and squalor with four or five siblings in a single room. Perhaps they worked for pitifully low wages as a shop girl or domestic servant. Men set upon them anyway, so they decided that they might as well receive payment for their favours. A common prostitute can earn in a night what she might otherwise earn in several weeks of honest labour. An uncommon prostitute can earn considerably more.

Prostitution was in full view in the 1830s in London. At the lowest level, frowsily dressed women walked the streets of poor neighbourhoods. They brought men to rooms for rent or performed their acts in alleys and other public places. The same women congregated in public taverns and foul dens where vice was closely packed and beds were available on the floor above or in a building nearby.

More presentable women also solicited in public. They were seen in carriages or leisurely strolling on promenades in the park, elegantly dressed, attracting attention by the striking colours and provocative cut of their attire. They wore satin bonnets trimmed with ribbons and ornamental flowers, their cheeks red with rouge as they flirted with their eyes. They could stare at a man in a way that was innocent yet inviting. By their walk, the manner in which they held their bodies, and their countless gestures, they could turn a man away or signal to him, "Yes, I am what you think I am."

They were a common sight at public events, these ladies. At dance halls and, most notably, at the theatre. They congregated at theatre bars and moved from box to box. In some theatres, it was understood that the upper tier was a place for solicitation. A woman who attended theatre alone was presumed to be a whore.

Some women of pleasure leave the trade to marry or pursue a different means of earning. But for most, prostitution is a slippery slope to a ruinous end. Syphilis and gonorrhoea are its twin plagues.

And there is a greater horror. Child brothels existed in London in the 1830s, often patronised because of the ignorant belief that sexual relations with a virgin would cure venereal disease. The age of consent in England was twelve. Many of the girls pressed into such service were twelve or thirteen. Some were eleven. Across the ocean in New York, the age of consent was ten.

Hortense Webster was disinterested in all of the common and uncommon forms of prostitution mentioned above. Her business was transacted out of public sight in the most exclusive kind of brothel, a private establishment known as The Abbey.

The Abbey was a three-story house in a good neighbourhood among private residences. It replicated an aristocratic club. The door was kept locked. Returning clientele and new gentlemen who came with a letter of reference were admitted.

Hortense's patrons were wealthy men, often married, who were willing to spend lavishly for beautiful women, luxurious surroundings, and discreet privacy. The most respectable men of London, including an occasional member of Parliament, made their way to her door.

Every furnishing and decorative touch in the parlour was designed to appeal to the senses, arouse desire, and remind guests that they were there to spend freely and have a good time. The walls were ornamented with hangings of rich silk on choice specimens of French paper, enriched with gilded cornices. Velvet curtains guarded the windows. Two ornate mirrors reflected the glow of candles. A dazzling crystal chandelier hung from above. Sofas and more intimate seating invited coupling. A plush carpet covered the floor.

An entry charge entitled each gentleman to a bottle of wine. More wine and champagne could be purchased by the bottle. Exquisitely prepared food was also sold. A man could go to The Abbey, eat and drink well, do no more than look at the women, and spend a princely sum.

Boisterous behaviour and vulgarity were not tolerated. No kissing or fondling was allowed in the parlour, which encouraged gentlemen to invite women upstairs. Companionship could be bought by the hour or for an entire night. If chosen, a woman could not refuse.

Eight prostitutes lived and worked in The Abbey. Over the years, Hortense's women had earned a well-deserved reputation for beauty. They were also educated in the art of conversation, flirtatious but refined. She dressed them in gowns of silk and fine linen, in colours that differentiated one from another at a glance, and in a style that accentuated each woman's most attractive physical qualities.

Hortense had never cared much for the physical demands of the trade, which she had practiced before becoming the proprietor of her own establishment. But the business side appealed to her. Her once-voluptuous figure had expanded so that her stomach was now as noteworthy as her bust. She walked on thin legs and wore long gowns that revealed as much of her breasts as possible and concealed the rest of her. She dressed in all black or all white with a great deal of powder and rouge and wore extravagant jewelry. Each night, sitting in the parlour, she surveyed her domain with pride.

Florence had long thought of herself as a low woman because of her degradation at the manor. Since that day, she had rebuffed all interest shown toward her by men. But three years in the dress shop had left her increasingly desperate regarding her circumstances. And Hortense Webster was kind to her.

Two months past her seventeenth birthday, Florence moved into The Abbey. Her room was on the third floor, furnished with a large bed, two chairs, and a dresser. A brick wall separated it from the room next door, which kept sound within her private space.

Hortense Webster introduced her to the other women and to the brothel staff. Cooks and waiters provided food and drink to the patrons. Maids cleaned rooms and brought fresh linen after each engagement. Two young men, well built and nicely dressed, served as guards.

"Think of the Abbey as a seminary for beautiful young women," Hortense told her.

Instruction followed.

Florence was taught how to dress and groom herself, the secret of every pin, string, and hook. She was counseled with regard to everything from proper manners to sexual technique.

She was to drink enough to entice a man to order more, but never to be drunk herself. If she was in the parlour with a man who was not ordering food or drink and she had the feeling that he would not pay for her services upstairs, she should delicately disengage while not offending him in a manner that led to unpleasantness.

Each patron was to feel that Florence was attracted to him and that he had a claim on some portion of her affections. If a gentleman gave her a piece of jewelry, it was hers to keep. But she must be wearing it when he returned.

The Abbey was safe from police intervention. To maintain that favoured position, it was essential that gentlemen not be unlawfully taken advantage of.

Hortense also gave Florence a tutorial on the use of protection fashioned from the intestines of sheep to avoid pregnancy and disease. Gentlemen were to be safely sheathed. One unfortunate encounter could leave her unclean for life . . . and render her useless to Hortense.

The women at The Abbey were business assets. As long as they separated men from large sums of money, they were fed well, nicely clothed, and sheltered. But if gentlemen stopped paying for a woman's services, she was let go. Whether her next work was in a less elegant private establishment, a public house, or an altogether different profession was of no concern to Hortense. Women she employed left her some times to marry or become mistress to a man they met at The Abbey. That deprived her of the whore's services and also a paying customer. If women could leave when it suited their purposes, there was no reason for Hortense to keep them on when they were of diminished use.

Florence's schedule was the same each day. Breakfast was served at eleven in the morning. The afternoon was hers to do with what she chose. Dinner was at five in the evening, dressing and make-up an hour later. Gentlemen began arriving at eight o'clock. The night's work ended two hours after midnight, when a light repast was served to the women.

Hortense decided that blue suited Florence best, and bought her two gowns in that colour. New women at The Abbey found themselves in demand for the sake of novelty, but Florence's beauty and manner attracted particular attention. On most evenings, she had two engagements. After each assignation, she bathed and cleaned herself. Once a month, a doctor examined her for signs of venereal disease.

The other women in the brothel were beautiful flowers. Florence befriended two of them. Elisabetta Landi was of Italian heritage with a radiant smile and a gift for playing the piano. Margaret Ellen was slender but shapely with fiery long red hair.

"You must never swallow," Margaret Ellen told Florence. "It will rot your teeth."

Florence was well paid. Her room was nicer than any she had lived in before. She bought occasional gifts for herself and put money aside for the future.

Her mind went elsewhere when she was with a gentleman. She smiled against her true feelings. Faces came and went. Some generous, some handsome, some kind, many the reverse. Each engagement was a source of suffering to her as it was of pleasure to the man. Each engagement brought back memories of that night at the manor when the master had his way.

There are no good prostitutes, Florence told herself, just as there are no black roses.

Not every gentleman who visited The Abbey went upstairs. Some could not afford it, were too shy, or came simply to eat and drink in a voyeuristic social surrounding. Most presented themselves as good and prosperous men. Some gave false names or none at all.

The tales they told about themselves were just as inventive as the tales told by the women.

A man came to the brothel. On the first night, he watched Florence with rapt attention. There was a moment when she sang while Elizabetta Landi played the piano. He watched her lips so closely that she was a bit afraid of him. It was as though he were kissing her as she sang. Thereafter, he brought small presents to her but never engaged her services upstairs. He was content to speak with her, eat and drink, and get to know the other gentlemen.

His name was Geoffrey Wingate. Several months after their dance began, he purchased Florence for an hour. They went to her room. She put her arms around him.

He awkwardly disengaged.

"There are things I must tell you. And then there is something I wish to ask."

Florence waited.

"I am different from the others. That part of me is never firm."

She said what she had been taught to say under those circumstances.

"I can pleasure you in other ways."

"That is not what I want," Wingate responded. "I have feelings for you. I do not wish to share you with others. I would like to take you away from this place to be my mistress. I will provide you with rooms of your own and a weekly allowance. I will treat you with respect and make few physical demands upon you."

Florence asked for a day to consider the offer. Wingate returned the following evening and purchased another hour of her time upstairs.

She had been at The Abbey for nine months. There was doubt in her mind as to how much longer she could endure the endless stream of men. Their heavy breathing and tongues, the groping of her breasts, the violation of her most sacred parts.

Geoffrey Wingate was offering a means of escape. She accepted his proposal.

A smile crossed his lips when Florence consented. Then he handed her a small box.

"Open it," he instructed.

Inside was a brooch fashioned in the shape of a rose. Red enamel on gold with a diamond in the center. Tiny pearls rimmed the edge of each petal. She had never seen jewelry so beautiful before.

"I will make you a lady," Wingate promised.

Society has found it convenient to distinguish between prostitutes and mistresses. In truth, when Florence fell under the dominion of Geoffrey Wingate, she simply became a whore for one man instead of many.

Wingate fulfilled his pledge. Three rooms, nicely furnished, were rented for Florence to live in. She was given a fixed allowance and gifts from time to time. She was expected to be at home when he called and to accompany him as required to dinner, theatre, and an occasional ball. He took her on trips outside of London, but never for more than several days. He made few physical demands upon her. She preferred it that way.

It was a fine thing for Florence to walk about the city with the key to her own home in her pocket. But she was no more in control of her destiny than she had been before.

Wingate moved quickly to form her character. He bullied and ordered: how to dress, when to speak, what to say. His word was law. There was to be a positive show of deference at all times in exchange for the advancement that he had given to her. He never struck her. But when he was angry, his touch left marks on her skin.

Florence tried to please him. "What I have learned from others," she said, "was only a prelude to what I have learned from you."

But he turned fondness to fear and duty to dread. She had been happier living behind the dress shop. The good whore was now a good slave. At times, he saw tears steal down her cheeks. But he never knew the cause, or cared.

"I am no longer fit for the world," Florence told herself. "Everything that purifies a woman's breast and makes it good and true no longer stirs in mine. I am lost. I have no hope at all. My heart is dead. There is only emptiness inside."

In one moment, everything changed.

Florence was walking alone on a sunny spring day in a part of London where merchants cater to the wealthy. Cloth from every quarter of the world was on display in shop windows. Ornately embroidered shawls from India, Chinese silks of the richest colours. And in the next window, exquisite vases and goblets, the finest bowls and plates.

Suddenly, Florence's breath grew short. Her knees trembled. Her heart beat so loudly in her chest that she feared it would stop beating.

A man was walking toward her on the street. He did not see her. He wore the clothes of a labourer. He was handsome and strongly made with long dark hair that fell in negligent waves. There was an air of ease and a natural grace about him. Heads turned as he passed, such was his presence.

He was James Frost.

They drew closer to one another. Their eyes met. Florence was sure that James saw her. A wave of shame swept over her. She had been defiled by the master, but that was little compared to the self-loathing she felt for her time at The Abbey and with Geoffrey Wingate. James was pure. She was a soiled woman and unworthy of him. There were no good whores. The life that Florence had lived degraded her in every eye that looked upon her. And she knew that James believed that to be so because, as their eyes met, he averted his at precisely the same moment that she averted her own in shame.

James saw her. He loved her as much as life itself and had for many years. But Florence was far above him now. He could see clearly by the manner in which she was dressed and the way she carried herself that she had ascended to a different class. She was a lady and he was a common labourer, unworthy of her. So he averted his eyes, knowing that he could look no longer without crying out her name. He did not know, and never had, why Florence fled the manor. He had prayed for years only that she was well and that he had done nothing to drive her away. She had seen him now. He knew that. And she had averted her eyes. He would do nothing to sully her life as a lady. So he walked on.

Florence thought only of James that night. She resolved that, in the morning, she would return to the place where they had passed. But as the sun rose, Geoffrey Wingate came unexpectedly to her door. He wished to go to the country.

Time passed with agonizing slowness for four long days. Minutes seemed like hours. There were many forced smiles from Florence and endless hidden tears. After what seemed to be an eternity, she and her overseer returned to London.

On the morning that followed, the face of Heaven shone bright and merciful.

James had gone each day to the street where Florence had appeared before him. If she came again, he would beg forgiveness for whatever part he had played in driving her from the manor. Even though she was now a lady, he would plead with her that he be allowed to occupy some small place in her heart.

Florence walked to where she had seen James. If only he were there, she would beg absolution for her sins and pray that, in some small way, he would take her back into his life.

There is no chasm, however deep and wide, that cannot be spanned by love.

Florence and James, with hearts pounding, once again saw each other. There was no mistaking their uncontrolled passion as they ran forward wildly into each other's arms. He drew her bosom close to his heart and pressed his lips against hers. She wept with joy. Without a word being spoken, they knew that they loved each other as much as it was possible for a man and woman to love.

Then they talked of old times and how their lives had been. James and Christopher had left the manor and journeyed to London together. They lived now under the same roof, doing honest labour when they could find it. They had been told little about why Florence fled. There were whispers that she had stolen gold coins and disappeared into the night. James did not believe that to be true. He hoped that Florence had not run away because he had frightened her with a kiss in the meadow.

Florence looked into James's eyes as he spoke those words, laughed, and kissed him again.

"I went away loving you. I stayed away loving you. I have loved you long and dearly. But I have fallen low. I have sold myself. I am a whore, a slut, a harlot."

Then Florence recounted for James her deflowering at the manor, The Abbey, and Geoffrey Wingate. He listened with tears in his eyes and, when she had finished, told her, "I cry for your suffering. As much as I loved you before, I love you more now. Never have I thought of you, nor do I think of you now, as anything but sacred and pure. You have been in every thought that I have had since we parted. You have been in every hope, every dream, in the clouds, the wind, the woods, and the sea. The stones that make the greatest churches in England are no more real than the thought of you has been to me."

At day's end, they pledged to meet again the following morning. That night, the stars seemed brighter and closer to earth than Florence had ever seen them.

There is no documented precedent of the sun having hastened its approach in response to one's wishes. Invariably, it rises to discharge its duty without being swayed by private considerations. Thus, morning came at its appointed time, although Florence wished it to come sooner.

James was where he had promised to be when Florence arrived for their rendezvous. Christopher was with him. Brother and sister embraced. The three were together for several hours. Then Christopher took his leave, so Florence and James could be alone.

They walked, but not on London's streets. It was through an enchanted city, where the pavement was of air, where rough sounds were softened into gentle music, where everything was happy and there was no distance or time. Sparkling jewels and gold flashed in shopkeepers' windows. Great trees cast a stately shade upon them. They walked lovingly together, lost to everything around them, thinking of no riches other than they now had in one another. Old love letters stored in boxes on dusty shelves might have stirred and fluttered as they passed by.

"The word that separates us shall never be said by me," Florence pledged. "You are my greatest and only love. I would not lose you for all the riches in the world. My heart is yours."

"If I were prosperous," James told her, "if I had any hope of one day being able to give to you that which you deserve, I would tell you that there is one name—that of husband—you might bestow upon me. I would tell you that I would honour it as a sacred trust above all others to protect and cherish you; that if given that trust, I would regard it as so precious that the fervour of my entire life would poorly acknowledge its worth. I long to defend and guard you. My whole heart is yours. But I am poor."

"Then let us be poor together. We will walk through country places as we did when we were young. We will wander wherever we wish to go, and sleep in fields and under trees, and never think of money. Let us rest at night and have the sun and wind upon our faces in the day and thank God that we are together. I am rich in joy and happy in every way being with you. I would rather pass my life with you and go out daily, working for our bread, than have the greatest fortune that was ever told and be without you. I want no fine clothes or jewels. I want no better home than you can give me. I only want to be with you. Let us be apart no longer. I have no hope of happiness but in you."

It was a lovely springtime evening. In the soft stillness of the approaching twilight, all nature was calm and beautiful. They came to a church, old and gray with ivy clinging to its walls.

James looked upon Florence's face with veneration and love, as though it were the face of an angel. Then he lowered himself to one knee.

"If you will consent to be my wife, I will love you dearly. I will go to the world's end without fear for you. I have nothing to give to you but my love. But my life shall be devoted to you, and with my last breath I will breathe your name to God."

"Rise up, fair prince. I want to be a better woman than I am and lead a blessed life as the wife of a good man. I will give to you openly in marriage the heart that you have so long owned."

The sun had dropped beneath the horizon, casting fading hues over the sky that spoke of its departure. James rose from his knee, and they embraced, as they had done many times that day.

"You were born to be a lady. And now you shall be mine, my lady. When shall I come for you?"

"I am appointed to see Geoffrey tonight. I will tell him and make ready for departure. Come for me at midnight."

James walked with Florence to her home. He knew now where to find her. They kissed once more, and he went away, promising to return at midnight.

She did not know that they would never part again.

Geoffrey Wingate arrived at Florence's residence at the customary hour. He took his seat at the dinner table, and she took hers. The meal had been prepared in haste.

There was awkward conversation as Florence sought to gather her courage.

"There is something I must tell you," she said at last. "I am unhappy in my circumstances."

"I have sensed it," Wingate told her. "I have thought about it and am amenable to a change. I wish to make you my wife."

In the entire time they had known each other, the word "love" had never been spoken between them. It was absurd. A bridal wreath would be a garland of steel spikes upon her head.

"I have the means to keep a wife well."

"I can never love you as you wish," Florence answered gently. "You do not know the heart of a young woman. I have no right to expect that you should. But when I tell you what I feel, I am sure that you will understand. I have thought night and day of ways to please you. I have gone on assuming the appearance of cheerfulness when my heart was breaking. Do not seek to find in me what is not there."

He leaned forward and stroked her hair. She recoiled at his touch.

"Have you formed another attachment?"

Florence's face grew red.

"There is someone from my childhood. He has awakened in me a dream of love and affection that I have never known."

"And you think that you were formed for one another like two pretty pieces on confectionery, do you?"

"My heart is set as firmly on him as ever the heart of a woman was set on a man. I have given it to him and will never take it back."

Wingate pressed his hands upon his temples. Then he rose from his chair.

"I command you to pleasure me."

"I cannot."

"Then I will speak to you plainly so there is no misunderstanding. Are you so foolish as to think that I have no feelings and you can simply cast me aside?"

Shame and passion raged within her. Every degradation that Florence had suffered swirled within like the dregs of a sickening cup. Throughout their knowledge of each other, her spirit had been down at Wingate's feet. She had obeyed his rules and never set her will against his. Now love emboldened her to say things bluntly that she might otherwise have not said.

"Do you think I love you? Did you ever care for my heart or propose to yourself to win the worthless thing? There is no slave at market, no horse in a fair, so shown and offered and examined and paraded as I have been these last shameful years. I have been hawked and vended until the last grain of self-respect was all but dead within me. You saw me at auction and thought it well to buy me. But I feel no tenderness toward you. You would care nothing for it if I did. And I know well that you feel none toward me."

He paced up and down the room several times with his hand positioned as if he were holding something, which he was not. A dark shade emerged from within him and overspread his face. Florence would long remember the look that he gave her, more like a murderer than a lover. Then his brow cleared, and he spoke gently.

"It would be better if you had only loved each other as boy and girl and left it at that. But what is done is done. Go with my blessing for the many happy hours that you have given to me and with my forgiveness for any pain you have caused. Go and have peace of mind. I wish only that you never hate me, that you think more fondly of me when you are no longer forced to wear the chain that I riveted around your neck. You leave me without blame."

As his voice softened, she responded in kind.

"I do not want to hurt you. I am sorry if I do. There are others who are far more worthy of your attentions than I. All the affection that I could find for you in my heart, I gave long ago. I have no more left to give you."

He nodded in understanding and then made a request:

"The rose that I gave you on the night that you became mine. If it is not too much to ask . . ."

He needed to say no more. Florence went to her bedroom, took the brooch from the drawer where she kept it safe, and brought it to him.

"I would like this man, whoever he is, to take you away this evening."

"It is already planned. He will come for me at midnight."

"Then it is all arranged. May you be happy in the life you have chosen."

After Wingate had gone, Florence filled two boxes with her belongings. She would leave behind the jewels and fine clothes that he had given her. It was only right that he should have them. And she wanted as few memories as possible of his presence in her life.

As for what happened next, I know some with certainty and can put together the rest through established facts and knowledge of human nature.

Wingate had seen the trembling on Florence's lips on their recent trip in the country but never suspected that a lover had won her heart. He imagined now two figures clasped in each other's arms while he stood above them, looking down. His wrath rose, flamed by his own impotence. The idea to shoot this other man seized him like a wild beast and dilated in his mind until it grew into a monstrous demon.

The evil deed was done from behind. The murderer stepped out of the shadows as James Frost approached Florence's home. Wingate did not have the courage to look James in the eye. James was given no opportunity to fight for his life. There was no grappling hand to hand. A shot was fired. A bullet lodged in the back of James Frost's head, and he fell to the ground, dead.

All of this was unknown to Florence as she waited for James to take her away. Tears of joy clouded her eyes. The best of her life lay ahead.

Wingate opened the door softy with a key and strode lightly up the stairs. Florence saw him. There was a dreadful look upon his face. Her own face was so beautiful, so full of dreams. His was a cruel mask.

He stared at her intently for several moments. His eyes looked powerfully down into hers. There was something ghastly in the contrast between the violent passion in them and his harsh low voice.

"You have brought this upon yourself. I hate with greater pleasure than I love."

Florence saw the bright sharp edge of a razor.

Wingate struck sharply. His hand was steady, and his thrust was deep. One motion, then another, slashing all trace of beauty from her. She staggered and fell blind in the eye that had been cut out by the razor as it sliced across her face. A face so beautiful moments before, now formless flesh and blood.

I sat, listening in horror, as Florence concluded her tale. Her face resembled the grotesque shaping of a wild painter's brush, not the work of Nature's hand.

"I had two eyes once. And my face was pretty. What happened can never be undone. But I am still a woman, one of God's creatures. Please, have the decency to look at me, Mr. Dickens."

CHAPTER 4

We sat close together. The glow of the fire cast a dim light on Florence's ruined beauty. As she told of the savagery that had befallen her and James Frost, her heart was so filled with grief that I thought I could hear it breaking. Death itself could not have been more sorrowful.

All the while, the baby lay sleeping with the innocent smile of childhood on its face.

James had been buried with a lock of Florence's hair tied to a ribbon placed round his neck. She had worn the ribbon on the day that they pledged their lives and their love to one another. It would lie upon his chest forever.

"Four years have passed since that day," Florence said as she told me of her journey. "Four years, and James has been with me ever since. In dark night and sun, in the light of candle and fire. No one has ever been happier than I was on our last day together. There was enough joy in those hours to keep me for this life on earth."

She held her hands tight upon her heart as she spoke, as if nothing less would keep it from splitting into small pieces.

"When I was a young girl, before I knew what death was, I would play in the churchyard with no thought to whose ashes lay beneath my feet. If you buried James fifty feet deep and took me across his grave, I should know without a mark that he was buried there. But he no longer lies in the grave. He has flown to a beautiful place beyond the sky where nothing dies or grows old. I hope he is as happy in his new life as I have prayed for him to be. And I wish that he has not given his heart to another, that he waits for me. I dream so much of Heaven and Angels and kind faces that I never see when I am awake. Heaven is a long way off, and they are too happy to come to the side of a poor woman like me. But in that other world, if I am forgiven my sins, I will wake some day and James will find me."

As Florence spoke, Christopher sat clenching his fist as if he were to beat down a lion.

"My sister was a toy for Wingate's pleasure," he said. "Let him remember what happened for so long as he is on this earth and for eternity in hell ever after."

"How did he escape punishment?"

"The word of a whore carries no weight against the word of a gentleman in an English court of law," Christopher said bitterly. "The police accepted a fiction he told and made threats against us should we pursue the matter."

"And you let it be?"

"I was of a mind to seek him out. Wingate was never in such peril of his life as he was at that time. When he is within five minutes of breathing his last, he will not be nearer to death than he was at my hand. But I feared punishment from the law that would deny Florence my protection. My curse is upon him. I still think of such an act. I wish he had never been born."

I wanted to know more about Wingate.

"How did he earn his pay when you knew him?" I asked Florence.

"He worked in business. That was all I knew."

"Did he work alone?"

"He had a partner whose name was Owen Pearce."

"How long were they partners?"

"Until Mr. Pearce died."

"There was more," Christopher urged his sister.

Florence worked her fingers together uneasily.

"I met Owen Pearce several times," she said at last. "We had dinner on occasion with Mr. Pearce and his wife. Her proper name was Lenora, but she preferred to be called Lily."

"Go on."

"After Mr. Pearce died, Geoffrey told me that Mr. Pearce had signed several documents in his presence. If I was asked about the matter, I was to say that I had been there when the documents were signed."

"What kind of documents?"

"I was told that it was none of my concern."

"How did you respond?"

"I understood the life I had. I gave for money what should only be given for love. And I knew nothing about business. But I would not have stories made for me and told him so. Geoffrey grew angry and said again that, were I asked, I should speak other than the truth."

The sound of the infant crying intruded on our conversation. Florence bent down over the egg crate and lifted up the child.

"What is her name?" I asked.

"Ruby."

"How old is she?"

"Seven months."

Pushing aside the ragged clothes that covered her breast, Florence began nursing her daughter.

"You are a gift to me, fresh from the hand of God. I should like it if, some day, you are a fine lady with a true love who shelters you in his arms. I live now so that some day you may be happy and remember a woman who looked over you and kissed you and called you my child."

Holding Ruby close, Florence turned toward me.

"Do not think that all power I had of loving is gone. I did not know that anything could be as dear to me again as she is now. It is not a slight thing when those who are so fresh from God bring us love."

Ruby stopped feeding, and Florence moved to put her down in the crate.

"May I hold her?" I asked.

Florence handed me her daughter. I cradled the baby in my arms. Words are not powerful enough to describe my emotions of that moment.

Ruby lay with her head upon my chest, her eyes trusting and wide, her soft cheek pressed against my heart. This child, as precious as any child born to rank and wealth, had a special grace about her. She clutched my shirt with a tiny hand, innocent of any knowledge beyond her immediate senses. I was completely at peace with myself. Every agitation and care passed from my soul. If I had died then with that feeling in my heart, I would have been more fit for Heaven than at any time in my life before or since.

"The light of intelligence is in her eyes," Christopher said. "I wish that she should be taught to read. There are times when I feel my want of learning very much."

Ruby fell asleep in my arms. Florence took her from me and set her down in the egg crate.

"There is not much cost to feeding her now. I just must keep my own condition strong. But before long, she will need more."

Night was approaching. I wanted to leave the slum before dark.

"There are several more questions I must ask. Do you know where I can find Lenora Pearce, the woman you knew as Lily?"

Florence shook her head.

"If it comes to pass that Wingate is placed on trial, would you be willing to bear witness against him in a court of law?"

"It would give me something more to live for."

"I will do what I can."

"It would be well if you could. Satan is in him. I ask myself at night some times if God is punishing me for giving myself to this man. I never walked the streets, but I was no better than those who do. Do you think I will suffer more in the afterlife for my wickedness?"

"God does not speak to me as he does to you, Miss Spriggs. But I believe that God is forgiving and understanding of all human conduct that flows from a person of tenderness. You should have no fear of what comes after the life that we know."

"In my dreams, I know that is true. I was beautiful once. Or so men said. In my dreams, some times, I am still beautiful."

"We must go now," Christopher told me.

He rose to lead me to the door. There was one thing more I wished to do. I reached into the pocket where I carried my coins and put them all in Florence's hand.

"For Ruby."

"Thank you. If there were more like you, there would be fewer like me. God bless you, Mr. Dickens."

❧

Christopher led me out of the slum by the same passage we had travelled before. The sun was fading, and the streets were more ominous than earlier in the day. Men and women dressed in rags huddled together in antici-pation of the night. They were of a class that works hard to stay alive, seeking no other destiny and having none.

A wretched woman stood at the entrance to an alley. Her face was wrinkled, her few remaining teeth pro-truded over her lower lip, and her bones were starting through her skin. She was singing a song of sorts in the hope of wringing a few pence from a compassionate passerby. A mocking laugh at her trembling voice was all she gained.

We passed a churchyard with straggling vegetation of the sort that springs up from damp and rubbish. No plant could have its natural growth as God designed it in that fetid bed. A new mound, not much longer than the body of an infant, had been freshly dug in the churchyard. Shrouds are not only for the old. They also wrap the young within their ghastly folds.

My thoughts went to Ruby and who her father might be. I wondered what would happen to her as she grew older.

Night came. The shadows were broad and black. Christopher lit an oil lamp that emitted a smokey yellow glow.

Two women emerged from the shadows. One was haggard with a lingering tinge of long-ago beauty. Something in her said without words, "I am younger than you would think to look at me." The other looked only of misery. She was the one who spoke.

"Put your hand under my dress. Touch me where I am wet. Only five pence each."

"Be gone with you," Christopher told her.

"Do you want me gone, sonny boy? Or would you rather my hand inside your britches?"

The streets were poorly lit with a spot here and there where lamps were clustered in a square or around some large building. Then the wind began to howl, and a heavy rain fell. Pools of water collected in deep brown mud.

Finally, we came to a place where I turned to Christopher and said, "I know the road from here. You need walk with me no further."

"Will you be safe?"

"There is nothing to be taken from me. My pockets are as empty as those of anyone I might pass."

We embraced.

"You have my word. I will do my best to bring you justice."

"Do that for my sister, and you shall not be friendless while I live."

I walked on alone through the cold wet streets of London. Before long, I was in a more decent part of the city where the street lamps were more frequent and shone more brightly. But I did not go home. Instead, I walked for hours in solitary desolation.

The rain stopped. The darkness diminished. There was no day yet in the sky. But there was day in the resounding stones of the streets, in the wagons and carts of labourers hurrying to work in pursuit of their family's daily bread.

The spires of churches grew faintly tinged with the light of the rising sun. Its beams glanced next onto the streets until there was light enough for men to see each other's faces. Church bells chimed, sharp and flat, muffled and clear. Those who had spent the night on doorsteps and stones rose and went off to beg. Shops opened. Commerce came to the markets.

All the while, I saw Florence Spriggs before me. I felt her suffering more deeply in my soul than all the suffering I had known or imagined before.

Wingate had cut her like meat and branded her with his hatred. He had taken the face that James Frost loved and turned it into a mask of horror. His unspeakable cruelty had deprived James of life and left his beloved with nothing more than the vision of a future that should have been and would never be.

A towering rage was building inside me. The flames kept rising. They would not subside. I made a vow.

If I did nothing more in my entire life, I would wreak Biblical justice upon Geoffrey Wingate and bring him to ruin.

Book 2

CHAPTER 5

I rested on the day after my journey into the slums of London. Then I confronted the issue of how to fulfill the pledge I had made to Florence and Christopher Spriggs. The best first step seemed to lie in bringing the matter to the attention of the police.

As I write these words in 1870, there is a unified, properly trained police force in London that serves as a model for police work throughout England. It was not always so. At the start of the nineteenth century, England relied on local watches and a parish constable system for the maintenance of order. As social and economic conditions changed, the machinery of law enforcement eroded. Crime grew rampant, particularly in London, and disorder was often prevalent.

Responding to the crisis, in 1829, Parliament passed the Metropolitan Police Act. There would be one police force in London, replacing the numerous inefficient local commands. The sole exemption from its jurisdiction was the original City of London—an area twenty blocks squared—that remained under the control of a command known as The City Police.

Headquarters for the new Metropolitan Police Force were established at Four Whitehall Place. The public was allowed to enter through a rear entrance on a street called Great Scotland Yard. The city was divided into seventeen districts, each having a superintendent, four inspectors, sixteen sergeants, and one hundred forty-four constables. Appointment to the force was by merit only. Constables were required to be under the age of thirty-five and at least five feet seven inches tall. A short hardwood truncheon was the only weapon they carried. The first recruits reported for training on 21 September 1829. On 25 September, night patrols began. Day patrols were instituted shortly thereafter.

Jurisdiction over the murder of James Frost and the mutilation of Florence Spriggs lay in the district where the crimes occurred. That was the station house I went to in the hope that my standing as a journalist would carry more weight than the word of a woman who had once practiced a less honourable profession. I stated my purpose to the constable on duty at the front desk and was brought to a small room upstairs.

The furniture was old. Stacks of papers were piled on shelves with tiers of boxes placed against the wainscot. Two desks with once-green baize tops that had grown withered and pale were in the center of the room. A man about thirty-five years of age sat behind one of the desks in a high-backed leather chair. He was stout with dark hair cropped close and intelligent eyes. Unlike the constable, who wore a dark blue long-tailed coat with blue pants, he was dressed in regular business attire.

The constable introduced the man to me as Inspector Benjamin Ellsworth and left the room. I recounted what I knew of the murder and slashing. Ellsworth listened with a reserved, thoughtful air. On occasion, he interrupted my recitation with a question, emphasizing his query with a forefinger put in juxtaposition with his eyes or nose. His manner was steady. I rather liked him.

"If I may ask," he inquired, "what is your interest in this matter?"

"My interest?"

"You have told me of a conversation you had recently with a woman who acknowledges that she was a prostitute. It is a horrifying tale, but I do not understand fully how you came to know her or what your motives are in pursuing the matter."

I explained as best I could my position as a reporter for *The Evening Chronicle*, how I had been asked to write about Geoffrey Wingate, and the investigation of his business affairs that led me to outrage.

Ellsworth rose from his chair and began rummaging through one of several boxes marked "1831." After a search of several minutes, he found what he was looking for, returned to his desk, and spread a sheaf of papers out in front of him.

"The incident occurred in spring 1831," he said, perusing the pages before him. "That was before I arrived in this district. The matter was investigated by Sergeant Bartholomew Dawes, who found that Florence Spriggs was the mistress of Geoffrey Wingate. James

Frost had known Miss Spriggs at an earlier time in their lives. In a fit of jealous rage, Mr. Frost inflicted horrible damage on the face of Miss Spriggs. Christopher Spriggs, the victim's brother, is believed to have shot Mr. Frost dead in retaliation. Sergeant Dawes spoke with a witness who saw a man whose description was similar to that of Christopher Spriggs running from the site of the murder. Sergeant Dawes said further that Mr. Wingate is a respectable gentleman and that he believed Miss Spriggs and her brother created a fiction after the murder and slashing in order to extort money from Mr. Wingate."

Rage underscored by the pounding of my heart coursed through my veins.

"That is an abomination."

"I understand your sentiments, Mr. Dickens. But as an inspector, I have been taught a simple rule. Take everything on evidence. Take nothing on its looks. Miss Spriggs may have a feel of honesty about her. But by her own admission, she practiced a trade that was dependent upon her ability to deceive men with regard to her true feelings and nature. You think that the study of facial expression comes by nature to you and that you are not to be taken in. That is an error. The fact that you give a great deal of time to the reading of Latin, French, whatever, does not qualify you to read the face of another. You cannot accept all that she tells you as truth."

It took a moment for me to gather my thoughts. Then I spoke.

"Florence Spriggs and Geoffrey Wingate are of different classes, but that is the least of their differences. They are as unalike as good and evil."

"Let me look further into the matter. If you return in two weeks time, I will tell you what I have learned."

After I left the station house, I made a decision that might have been foolish. Fueled both by outrage and a reporter's curiosity, I felt compelled to visit Geoffrey Wingate.

The most common form of public transportation in London is the omnibus, a vehicle drawn by horses that follows a given route. Passengers get on and off as often as the patterns change in a kaleidoscope, although they are not as glittering and attractive.

I disembarked the omnibus near Wingate's residence, walked the final two blocks, and made several turns in the street with the hesitation of a man who is conscious that the visit he is about to pay is unexpected and might also be unwelcome. Finally, I approached the front door, grasped the brass lion's head that guarded the house, and slapped it firmly against wood.

A servant opened the door. I handed him my card.

"Would it be possible for me to have a few minutes with Mr. Wingate?"

"Do you have an appointment, sir?"

"No. But we have met before."

I was escorted into the foyer. Several minutes passed. The servant returned with Amanda Wingate.

"Mr. Dickens, it is so nice to see you. To what do we owe this unexpected pleasure?"

"I thought I might speak further with your husband

about his business. I can come back another time if it is
inconvenient for Mr. Wingate to see me now."

Amanda brought me to the parlour, waited until I
was comfortably seated, and disappeared from view.
"Geoffrey is with a client," she said on her return. "But
if you join me for tea, he will be available in less than
an hour."

All the while, she stood perfectly erect, her figure
drawn up to its full height. She was the most beguiling
woman I had ever seen. As on the day when we met, her
clothes had a certain character of tightness, as though
everything with two ends that were intended to unite
were such that the ends were never on good terms and
could not quite meet without a struggle. There was an
untamed quality about her.

Tea was served.

"I read several of your sketches this past week,"
Amanda told me. "I admire those who excel in the art
of writing."

We talked for a while about Boz. Then I led the conversation in a different direction.

"When did you and Geoffrey meet?"

"Three years ago."

"How long have you been married?"

"It will be two years next month."

She deflected further questions about herself, always
bringing the conversation back to me. At one point, her
lady's maid came into the room. Amanda introduced
us almost as equals. Clarice, the maid, was appropri-
ately deferential. I liked the fact that Amanda treated
her as she did.

In due course, another servant appeared and announced that Wingate would see me in his office.

I sat in the same seat that I had occupied three weeks earlier.

"I hope that I am not intruding."

"Not at all," Wingate said with a smile.

I could not say much against his features separately. But put together, I no longer liked their look. His smile, it now seemed, did not extend beyond his mouth, so there was something in it like the snarl of a cat.

"I am curious as to how you began in business," I asked.

"I was brought into finance by a man named Owen Pearce. He taught me what he knew, and I became his partner."

"What brought the partnership to an end?"

"He died."

I looked closely at the character in Wingate's face. Calculation was ever present in his eyes.

"How did he die?"

"Under unfortunate circumstances. It was a great loss. To have had him as a partner and friend for as long as I did was a blessing in my life."

I cautioned myself that Benjamin Ellsworth had questioned the credibility of Wingate's accusers. That did little to put my prejudices to rest.

We spoke more about his business. Either Wingate was speaking differently from the way he had spoken during our first interview, or my ears were attuned to different things.

"There are times when I am subtle. I am often diplomatic. But I am never dishonest . . . Envious people some times speak against me, but things roll on just the same . . . Do you know what rumour is, Mr. Dickens? It is idle gossip. One should never repeat rumour. That is the only way of paring the nails of the rumour monster."

For the most part, Wingate looked steadily into my face. Once, he rose from his desk, put his hands in his pockets, rattled the money that was in them, and laughed. Finally, he dipped his pen into the inkstand on his desk and began to write. It was a signal that our meeting was over.

Then he said something that surprised me.

"Amanda and I are entertaining for dinner at six o'clock on Saturday evening. If you have no better engagement, it would give me great pleasure if you and your betrothed could join us."

The advantages in accepting Geoffrey Wingate's invitation to dinner seemed to outweigh their negative counterparts. So on behalf of Catherine and myself, I accepted.

Catherine had heard Wingate's name mentioned by her father and, when told of the evening's plans, was excited by the prospect of sharing a meal in such fine company. I thought it best not to enlighten her with regard to my beliefs as to our host's character.

On Saturday evening, we rode by hackney carriage to the Wingate home. A servant opened the door and took our coats. Geoffrey, as we were instructed to call him, greeted us warmly.

"I hope you have brought your appetite with you."

We sat first in a large room with a fireplace that radiated warmth. The furniture had an air of old-fashioned comfort. Crimson drapery hung from the windows. Candelabras twisted like the branches of trees stuck out from richly paneled walls. Every ornament was in its place. Decanters stood filled with fine Scotch whiskey, sherry, and wine.

The other guests were Cedric Baldwin, August Rutledge, and their wives.

Cedric arrived wearing an extremely stiff hat, which looked as though it would sound like a drum if struck with the knuckles. He was a short pudgy man with a shiney bald forehead and deep voice of which he seemed uncommonly proud. His lineage was such that he had been surrounded by wealth from the cradle, and he spoke as though descended in a direct line from Adam and Eve. I learned that it was a source of great comfort and happiness to him that, in various periods of recorded history, his forbearers had been actively connected with numerous slaughterous conspiracies and bloody frays and that, being clad from head to heel in steel, they did on many occasions lead their leather-jerkined soldiers to the death with invincible courage and afterward returned home to their relations and friends.

August was a tall thin man with a profusion of brown hair, the neck of a stork, and the legs of no animal in particular. His skin was so pale that, were he cut, I believe he would have bled white. The least of his stories had a colonel in it. Lords were more plentiful than commoners.

The two wives, named Juliet and Grace, were richly dressed in silk and satin with glittering jewels on their fingers, wrists, and neck. Catherine's ring was quite modest by comparison, composed of not much diamond and a great deal of setting.

Wingate introduced me to the others as "the man who is Boz." Catherine imparted the information that I had recently moved into new rooms in anticipation of our marriage. Cedric praised our host's business acumen, informing everyone present, "I've invested thirty thousand pounds with him. His methods are safe and certain." August opined, "They say that virtue is its own reward. But as a man of business, I prefer monetary compensation."

Amanda was gorgeously attired in a manner that flaunted the superiority of her charms. As before, her clothes were of a tight-fitting fashion. The evening dress she wore was a tantalizing shade of green, pulled in to accentuate the smallness of her waist with beads aligned on the silk in such a way as to draw one's eye to her generously exposed bosom. As if one needed prompting.

A gold bracelet, dangling gold earrings, a diamond ring. She was a magnificent work of art to hang jewels upon. Dazzling, striking, tall, and stately. Dignity and grace were in her every movement. In an unguarded moment, I saw Wingate looking at her as a man might look at a resplendent tiger in its cage.

Then it was time for dinner. The dining room was remarkable for the splendour of its appointments. The table was busy with glittering cutlery, plates, and glasses. A half-length portrait in oil of our host hung on a wall opposite the windows. Artists on commission always make their subjects out to be more handsome than they are, or they would get less work. Such was the case here.

The feast began. Sumptuously cooked dishes were elegantly served. A roast leg of pork bursting with sage and onion. A stuffed filet of veal with thick rich gravy. Vegetables and breads. Exquisite wine.

"Geoffrey is a wonderful judge of wine," Amanda told us.

When not otherwise engaged, the butler stood by the sideboard. From the servants I saw that evening and from conversation at the table, I gathered that Wingate had a staff of eight in his employ. There was the butler, a valet, Amanda's lady's maid, a housekeeper, a cook, a young woman who assisted the housekeeper and cook, an errand boy, and a man who performed the tasks of coachman, stable master, and gardener.

When asked, Catherine offered the information that she was the oldest of nine children. Throughout her life, she was inclined toward corpulency and over-eating. On this occasion, she blushed very much when anybody was looking at her and ate very much when no one was looking. The veal on her plate disappeared as if the poor little calf still had the use of its legs.

She also drank too much wine, and I wished that she would refrain from speaking on any but the most mundane subjects. Then she drank more, and I concluded that her merits would show to the greatest advantage in silence.

Amanda distributed her attention among all of the guests. Each person had her full attention while they were engaged. She adapted her conversation with graceful instinct to the knowledge of others, beginning on a subject that the guest might be expected to know best. She understood just enough of each person's pursuits as made her agreeable to that person and just as little as made it natural for her to seek information when a theme was broached.

She was enviably self-possessed, enchanting in the politeness of her manner, the vivacity of her conversation, and the music of her voice.

The conversation turned to the condition of society, and I found myself discoursing on the monstrous neglect of education in England and the disregard of it by the government as a means of forming good or bad citizens and miserable or happy men. That led to a discussion of differences in class.

"The classes must be joined with an understanding of the bonds that exist between them," I said. "The rich and powerful owe an obligation to the poor. In a just society, the fate of all would be intertwined."

"And what do you mean by that?" August Rutledge demanded.

"The strengthening of England lies in the fusion of the classes, in the creation of a common understanding. A true aristocracy would be comprised of those who earn their place in it through hard work, intelligence, and virtue."

That brought Wingate into the conversation.

"Life is a serious game," he said. "Everybody is playing against you. Wealth must defend itself."

"Rich and poor are equal as they lie dreaming in bed," I countered. "Virtue shows quite as well in rags as it does in silk."

As I spoke those words, Cedric Baldwin made a show of yawning. "I am not a scholar," he declared. "But I am a citizen of England. It is in vogue in some circles to talk about the plight of the poor. However, the work houses solve the problem."

For reasons unbeknownst to me, Catherine chose that moment to enter the conversation.

"I think it best if church and charity care for the poor and leave the government to fighting wars and whatever else it does best."

Wingate smiled at me. "Your bride-to-be is as intelligent as she is beautiful."

"It is possible that the flavour of sour grapes is in Mr. Dickens's mouth," Cedric Baldwin added.

Then something totally unexpected happened.

"I think that Mr. Dickens's position is admirable," Amanda snapped. "If you had been born to less wealth, perhaps you would feel differently about the matter."

There was fire in her eyes.

"You, sir," she said, addressing Baldwin, "are a coal merchant. The men who toil in your mines and their families know a different world from yours. Their children are not taught to read. There is no hope for a better life. And those are the families where there are men living in the home and the men have work. There is far worse suffering in England."

"It is of little importance to me how the poor live."

"Perhaps not. But it is of importance to them."

Throughout the conversation, the other wives had remained silent. Now Juliet Baldwin intervened.

"The poor would be less of a problem if there were fewer of them. They have no business being born. They have boys who grow up bad and run wild in the streets, and girls who breed more children who, like their parents, should never have been born."

Amanda fixed a withering gaze upon her.

"I am of the belief, Mrs. Baldwin, that the poor were made by a higher intelligence than yours."

The remembrance of Amanda and how she spoke in those moments remains with me to this day. She glowed more gloriously than fire.

"Let us avoid these morsels of morality," Wingate said, seeking to defuse the situation.

"I will speak as I choose," Amanda told her husband.

"Keep a watch upon yourself."

"I shall not. The conditions of which Mr. Dickens speaks exist. And no nation that allows them to exist is fully civilised."

"Is that all?" Cedric Baldwin inquired with a note of levity in his voice.

"Yes, sir. That is all. And enough, too, I think. I would prefer not to regard you as hard-hearted."

"It will all be the same and make no difference a hundred years from now," Wingate said, continuing his efforts to move the conversation away from conflict. "In the graveyard, we are all alike."

His voice was such that it travelled from melodious to harsh as befitted his mood. Now it was at its most engaging. "I propose a toast to Mr. Dickens and his future bride. May this be the dawn of happy days for both of you."

The dinner ended soon after.

"I like this sort of thing," our host told us. "I hope all of you do not mind dining at another man's expense."

"Not at all," Baldwin offered.

"Then I trust you will dine with us often."

All that was left was for Wingate to walk Catherine and myself to the door.

"The great thing is to be on the right side," he said, laying a hand upon my shoulder. "We are not as different from one another as you might pretend. Be one of us."

A hackney carriage brought Catherine and myself to our respective homes, stopping first at her father's residence and then my own. It was a lumbering square vehicle with small windows. The straw with which the seating cushion was stuffed protruded from the canvas in several places.

"You spoke inappropriately tonight," Catherine chided as the carriage neared her father's residence.

"I did not."

"You were needlessly confrontational, and you flirted with Mrs. Wingate for the entire evening."

"That is untrue."

"It is perfectly true. I had my eye upon you the whole time."

I was unsure as to what I should say next and uncertain whether the carriage ride would end with my being embraced or scratched. Either possibility seemed equally disagreeable.

The preceding days had brought turmoil to my emotions. The visit to Florence Spriggs and all that surrounded her had taken my thoughts back to the year I had spent in the blacking warehouse. With that came ruminations on the uncertainties of fate and the thin line that separates one kind of life from another.

More unsettling, I was aware that, during the conversation at dinner, Amanda Wingate and I had been more as husband and wife should be in their thoughts than Catherine and I had been.

CHAPTER 6

Shortly after Catherine and I dined at the Wingate home, I posted a letter to Geoffrey thanking him for a lovely evening and offering assurances that I still intended to make him the subject of a sketch by Boz. My work at Doctors' Commons had acquainted me with certain aspects of finance and law. But after further investigation of Wingate's dealings, I understood only that there was a business in which people invested money and Wingate then reinvested their money in various financial instruments by means of a complicated series of assignments, conveyances, purchases, and settlements.

Meanwhile, there were reporting duties to discharge at *The Evening Chronicle*, and I was writing the first installment of *The Pickwick Papers*.

Two weeks after my meeting with Benjamin Ellsworth, I went back to the station house as he had suggested. I

expected little or no satisfaction. Ellsworth came down-
stairs to greet me and introduced me to Bartholomew
Dawes, whose name I recognised as the constable
whose report had exonerated Wingate of the horrific
crimes committed against Florence Spriggs and James
Frost.

Dawes was heavily moulded with half-whiskers, a
sallow complexion, and dark eyes set deep in his head.
The yolk of an egg had run down his coat, and yolk of
egg does not match any coat but a yellow coat, which his
was not. I saw also that he had a gold pocket watch and
ring of a kind beyond what one would expect his station
in life to warrant. He made it clear in greeting me that
a smile was not part of the bargain for his salary.

There is a vast quantity of nonsense about how a bad
man will not look you in the eye. I do not believe that
convention. Dishonesty will stare honesty out of coun-
tenance every day of the week if there is anything to be
gained by it. That said, Dawes and I were introduced,
and our mutual inspection was brought to a close when
he averted his eyes.

Ellsworth led me upstairs to his office and offered me
a chair opposite his desk. There were more papers than
had been there before. Otherwise, the room seemed
unchanged. We were alone.

"I have been to see Miss Spriggs," he said.

I had not expected that.

"How did you learn where she lives?"

"I have my ways. I am not as slow of mind as you
might think me to be."

"How do you view the situation?"

"Miss Spriggs spoke in a manner bearing the imprint

of truth," the inspector answered. "I told her that I could make no promise regarding the outcome of the investigation, but that I will pursue the matter."

"What will you do next?"

"I have located Lenora Pearce, the widow of Geoffrey Wingate's deceased business partner. She lives several hours north of London. The authorities there have arranged for me to visit her on Friday of this week."

Ellsworth paused, as though weighing a matter of importance, which is precisely what he was doing.

"You may accompany me if you wish."

The offer was unexpected—a fact that I conveyed to him in the same breath as my acceptance.

"I have learned to trust my instincts and do things in unconventional ways," he said. "But our conversations are not for the newspaper. Is that understood?"

"Yes."

"Clearly understood."

"Yes."

"Very well, then. Meet me outside the main entrance to police headquarters at Four Whitehall Place on Friday morning at ten o'clock. It would be best if you refrain from discussing this matter with anyone. Including Constable Dawes."

❦

Throughout my life, I have been habitually early, particularly in matters of travel. Benjamin Ellsworth shared that trait. He was waiting when I arrived at Four Whitehall Place on Friday twenty minutes before the appointed hour.

There were no other passengers on the stagecoach as we journeyed north, which allowed us to speak freely.

"My father was a footman," Ellsworth told me. "Then a butler, then an innkeeper. He lived universally respected and died lamented. He said often to me that service is an honourable career."

Bit by bit, the inspector revealed more about himself and asked questions that explored my own character. Then the conversation changed.

"I had best prepare you for our meeting with Lenora Pearce," he said as we neared our destination.

I waited for what would come next.

"Owen Pearce was shot dead on the street at night after leaving the office that he shared with Geoffrey Wingate. The authorities were brought in and took possession of his body. His wallet and watch were missing. The motive was presumed to be robbery."

I sat still.

"The similarity between the deaths of James Frost and Owen Pearce and the fact that Geoffrey Wingate can be linked to both men raises an obvious inference," the inspector continued. "Unfortunately, inference falls short of proof. The science of police work is evolving. In the not too distant future, we will have a class of detective police skilled in science and deductive reasoning. Some day, I believe, we will be able to assign guilt by studying the tips of men's fingers and the bullets used in the commission of crimes. But we have not yet realised that goal."

Lenora Pearce lived in a little market town with two churches separated by a winding river. The journey from London took just under three hours. When we arrived, Ellsworth announced, "Appetite is the best clock in the world." The next forty minutes were devoted to his clock.

In due course, we made our way to Lenora Pearce's home. It was a neat little house with a room in front for reception and a small back room for sleeping. The furniture was simple. A few rough chairs, a table, and a corner cupboard in one room. A small bed and chest of drawers in the other. Adornments had been placed throughout the house and arranged in such a manner that the effect was charming. The fireplace was old and paved at the sides with tiles meant to illustrate the scriptures. Three little white crockery poodles, each with a black nose and a basket of flowers in its mouth, stood guard on the mantel shelf.

Mrs. Pearce was a woman of orderly appearance, who looked about forty years old. Her dress was sewn where it had been torn, and her shoes were mended.

"Do not be alarmed by our presence," Ellsworth told her. "You have done nothing wrong. We are here seeking information with regard to the death of your husband. It is possible that you may be able to cast light upon things that are presently dark for us."

"It is all dark," Lenora Pearce responded. "Do you know what it is to lose a husband?"

"Never having had a husband, or a wife for that matter, I do not know what it is to lose one. But a great deal depends on your willingness to answer the questions that I ask of you."

She had sad eyes. There was no pretence in her face.

"I would like to know of your husband's relationship with a man named Geoffrey Wingate."

Lenora Pearce's body stiffened, and the sad eyes turned angry.

"He acted the gentleman when my husband first knew him, with his proper clothes and fancy airs. I know him now for what he is—a villain who hid behind a mask of friendship. In Wingate's mind, the whole great sky at night glitters with sterling coin. Money is all that matters to him. He should be compelled to swallow every coin in England until he chokes to death."

Ellsworth took a pencil and small notebook from an inside coat pocket.

"Tell me more. A very little key can some times open a heavy door."

A sad recitation followed.

Owen Pearce was born in London in 1790. He was a man of distinguished appearance with the integrity of an honest cleric and the manner of a good school teacher. His chosen profession was the raising of capital for public companies.

Lenora was six years younger than her husband. They married in her twentieth year and had two children, a boy and a girl. Both children died young.

In 1820, a young man named Geoffrey Wingate came to London from the southwest corner of England. He met and was employed by Owen Pearce.

Pearce taught Wingate all that he knew about business. His pupil discarded the teachings that had to do with ethics and used the rest to his advantage. The realisation of this did not come to Pearce until it was too late. In 1827, he extended an offer of partnership to Wingate that was quickly accepted.

Over time, the older man came to doubt the wisdom

of his decision. Wingate did things differently in his position of partnership from the way in which he had done them before. He considered himself to be free of restraints. Bluntly put, his integrity was in question. Pearce told his wife that he planned to terminate the partnership. One week later, Owen Pearce was found near the Thames River with a bullet in his head.

The murder occurred in January 1831. Wingate handled all of the funeral arrangements. Then he produced a partnership agreement between Pearce and himself that gave the entire business to the surviving partner in the event that one of them died. Equally devastating, Pearce had purchased an assurance policy on his life that named his estate as the recipient of all payments. Wingate revealed the existence of a later-signed document that purported to make him the beneficiary.

It was then that Lenora Pearce became acquainted with the majesty of the law. There are many pleasant fictions in English jurisprudence. None is so pleasant or fictitious as the supposition that every person is of equal value in its impartial eye and that its protection is available to all. Almost always, matters of law are reduced to matters of business. There is a great deal of form but, often, little truth.

The treatment of Owen Pearce's estate and related matters was a monstrous wrong from beginning to end. There were bills, cross-bills, answers, rejoinders, affidavits, masters' reports, technicalities, trickery, evasion, slippery precedents, and false pretences.

The law might have been on Lenora's side, but the judges were not. Wingate was awarded the assets of the partnership and most of the assurance money. Lenora received what remained of her husband's estate. Unable to pay her bills in London, she returned to the town of her birth. She never heard from Wingate again.

Ellsworth listened as Lenora recounted her losses.

"I wish to ask you," he said when she was done. "You said that your husband questioned Wingate's integrity. You have every reason to do so now. What were the reasons for Mr. Pearce's suspicions?"

Lenora shook her head.

"I do not know. I can only tell you that Owen was troubled by several things that he learned. He considered bringing Wingate's conduct to the attention of the authorities but decided to terminate the partnership and leave the rest alone."

"Do you have any papers that relate to what we have discussed?"

"No."

Ellsworth put his pencil back into its sheath and returned it with the notebook to his coat pocket.

"You have been shamefully treated," he told her. "I would ask in a positive way that you not be unmindful that you are blessed with good health. As for Wingate, he will not be rid of me so easily as he has been of others. I promise you that."

"He has the heart of a serpent," Lenora responded with anger in her voice. "If I had a dagger and he was within my reach, I would place it in his false mean heart."

"Don't be doing that, ma'am."

"And then I would put him in a sack with a hundred venomous snakes and throw the filth in the river."

Ellsworth was silent as we began our ride back to London.

"Nothing bears so many stains of blood as gold," he said at last. "It is sad to contemplate what a man may do within the law and beyond it."

He paused before continuing his thoughts.

"There is also the death of James Frost. We do not know that Wingate was responsible for both murders. Of course, we do not know that the earth will last another hundred years. But it is highly probable that it will."

He took his notebook from his coat pocket and began studying the notes he had made.

"We have two murders . . . a vicious assault that disfigured a woman . . . the likelihood of forged documents . . . These are serious charges. And I believe that some, if not all of them, are true. What leads a man to deeds like this? Greed? Hatred? Anger?"

During the time that Ellsworth had taken notes in Lenora Pearce's home, I was not idle in the matter, having brought my stenographic book. Now, sitting in the coach with the inspector, I read aloud portions of his conversation with Lenora.

"That can be useful," he said thoughtfully. "I will remember that you have this skill."

It was dark by the time we arrived in London.

"Feel free to further investigate Geoffrey Wingate's present financial company but nothing more," Ellsworth instructed. "If you find anything of importance, communicate it directly to me. Not to Bartholomew Dawes."

I nodded in understanding.

"I was not a believer in the old police," Ellsworth said, removing all doubt as to the meaning of his admonition. "Many of them were of questionable ability and character. Constable Dawes is left over from the previous way of doing things. I fear that he is not a moral man."

We said good night on the street where our day's journey had begun.

"There are times when life is sloppier than one expects to find it," Ellsworth said in parting. "We have come upon unsettling circumstances. Only God knows how this will end."

CHAPTER 7

On Monday, the fourteenth of March, three days after Benjamin Ellsworth and I visited Lenora Pearce, another sketch by Boz appeared in *The Evening Chronicle*. It was not about Geoffrey Wingate. Rather, I wrote about a shopkeeper and the more mundane aspects of life in London.

Late in the afternoon, I was in my lodging. Myriad thoughts were swirling through my mind. The first installment of *The Pickwick Papers* was scheduled for publication at the end of the month. I could not separate my thinking from Florence Spriggs, James Frost, and Owen Pearce. In nineteen days, Catherine Hogarth would become my bride. The emotions that she was engendering in me compared unfavourably with those expressed in Shakespeare's sonnets. And I was having visions. Fragments of novels that, with the grace of God, I would write some day were dancing in my brain. Street urchins, kings and queens, beautiful women, evil dwarfs.

A rapping on the door intruded upon my thoughts. I opened it and stood opposite one of Geoffrey Wingate's servants.

"Mr. Charles Dickens?"

"I am Dickens."

"Mr. Wingate asked that I bring this letter to you and wait for your reply."

He handed me an envelope. The letter inside had an embellishment at the top not unlike a family coat of arms and was written in a strong, slanted hand:

Dear Mr. Dickens,

   I trust this note finds you well.

   Mrs. Wingate and I were planning to attend the ballet on Thursday evening of this week. Unfortunately, I find that I have a pressing business engagement that must take precedence.

   Amanda tells me that she enjoyed your company when you dined at our home and suggested that I ask whether you would be so kind as to accompany her to the ballet in my absence. Please advise my coachman of your availability. If you are able to attend, he will be at your service on Thursday evening.

                                 Very truly yours,

                                 Geoffrey Wingate

I knew at once that I would go.

It was not because I was a reporter for *The Evening Chronicle* with a professional interest in Geoffrey Wingate. Nor was it because I was engaged in the pursuit of justice on behalf of people who had been horribly wronged. I wanted to see Amanda Wingate again.

I wrote a note of acceptance and gave it to the coachman. He told me the time at which he would come for me on Thursday. I waited through the next three days with anticipation, and on the evening of the ballet, rode in the carriage to Geoffrey Wingate's home with excitement and a bit of apprehension.

A servant met me at the door. Amanda came into view before I entered. She had a proud and willful demeanor that was inseparable from her beauty. Diamonds, bright and sparkling, hung round her neck. Her coat concealed the attire that lay beneath, but I knew by now that she had a love of display and was fond of silk and satin. She knew she was beautiful. How could she not? It was impossible for a woman to have more beauty.

We got in the carriage. Young men were lighting lamps in the street as we passed by.

"You are beginning to be famous," Amanda said at the start of our conversation. "I have never known a man who had his words published before. And you have passion for the poor. I admire that."

We talked of the need to treat people with respect regardless of their class. That the same qualities, good and bad, that are in the finest of lords are also found in England's least fortunate citizens.

When I think now of that night, it comes back to me as if in a dream. We ride past people who are closing their shops and returning to their homes from their daily work. Amanda looks more beautiful than I have seen her before. She is a treasure fit for a king. I know that she is to be looked at and on no account to be touched. But when we arrive at the Theatre Royal at Covent Garden, she steps from the carriage and puts her arm through mine.

A strange sensation sweeps through me. We enter the hall. Amanda removes her coat. She is dressed in lavender-coloured silk fashioned in a way that accentuates her charms and ensures that she will receive maximum admiration.

I walk with her down the aisle. She carries herself with grace, moving through the crowd as though she has been lifted onto a pedestal to be seen. All eyes are attracted as though there is a magnetic field about her. Elegant gentlemen and richly dressed ladies praise her beauty in whispers as we pass. She is enchanting and out of reach of ordinary mortals. Yet I am walking with her.

I have been to the ballet many times since then, but never free of that night. There was music and a great stage with people dancing upon it. Graceful figures twirled round and round in airy motion, spreading like expanding circles in water. It was a magical evening. I was immensely happy.

The theatre was well filled. At the end of the performance, the people poured cheerfully out. As we returned to the Wingate home in the carriage, I wished that the road could be stretched out to a hundred times its natural length.

"How did you and Geoffrey meet?" I asked.

"At a dinner party. I was nineteen at the time. We married a year later."

I decided to probe a bit.

"Has his business changed since then?"

"I know that Geoffrey is a brilliant man of business, but I have no understanding of that world."

I asked where she had been born and the circumstances of her earlier life. She deflected the questions skillfully, as though it was a game she had played before. Finally, she said simply, "My way has been through paths that you will never tread. It would be of little interest to you, Mr. Dickens."

"But it is."

"Then it is none of your concern. No further inquiries are necessary."

We returned to more harmonious conversation. I looked up at a star in the sky that was brighter than any of the others. Amanda's waist was made for an arm such as mine. Her face would be in my dreams.

The carriage arrived at Amanda's home. I escorted her to the door. And my heart sank.

I had not seen it earlier in the evening. Now I did and knew immediately what it was. A brooch fashioned in the shape of a rose was pinned to Amanda's coat. Red enamel on gold with a diamond in the center. Tiny pearls rimmed the edge of each petal.

"A lovely piece of jewelry," I said.

"I'm glad you like it. Geoffrey gave it to me on the night that he proposed marriage."

She wished me a good night and held out her hand with a dignified air. I kissed it.

"Your acquaintance is of great pleasure to me, Mr. Dickens. My coachman is at your service to take you home."

My mind was filled with conflicting thoughts as the carriage made its way through the streets of London to my quarters. I knew that I should have one set of feelings, yet I felt another.

I had no way of knowing the extent to which Amanda was aware of her husband's conduct. Certainly, she did not know of the brooch's provenance. She could not know, I told myself.

The carriage arrived at Furnival's Inn. I took uneasy notice of the shadows that protruded onto the street. Other men in Geoffrey Wingate's orbit had been struck down at night by a bullet in the head.

Once I was in my rooms, the fear passed, and I thought again of Amanda. She was temptation beyond reach. And yet . . .

I knew it was wrong. I knew that I should not allow it to happen. I whispered to myself that I must not think of such a thing. But I was falling in love with Amanda Wingate.

CHAPTER 8

My evening at the ballet with Amanda was very much in
my thoughts in the days that followed. I saw no need to
tell Catherine about it. Nor did I tell anyone else.

In addition to my regular reporting duties for *The
Evening Chronicle*, I continued to investigate Geoffrey
Wingate's business empire. When time allowed, I went
to various records offices and spoke to innumerable
clerks. The sum total of what I learned amounted to
between little and nothing.

Benjamin Ellsworth had instructed me to limit my
investigation to Wingate's ongoing financial empire.
I decided to ignore his edict and learn what I could
about Owen Pearce. The record of Pearce's marriage
was where I expected it to be. But the file relating to his
will and the assurance policy on his life was missing at
Doctors' Commons.

Ellsworth had also instructed me to communicate directly with him if I learned anything of importance. I decided to follow that much of his edict, and on the last Monday in March, I went to the station house to advise him of the missing file.

The inspector greeted me with a handshake. We went upstairs to his office, and he offered me a chair. I told him of the missing file, and he pointed to the papers on his desk.

"The file is there," he said.

I expected that revelation to be followed by a repri-mand for disobeying his orders. Instead, he thumbed through the papers, recounting what he had learned.

"The policy on Owen Pearce's life was with the London Assurance Company in the amount of ten thousand pounds. The premium was paid from year to year. After Pearce died, documentary evidence was sub-mitted to the court in support of the proposition that the deceased had changed the policy beneficiary from his wife to Geoffrey Wingate. The judge, for reasons that are unclear to me, ruled in Wingate's favour."

"Wingate also gave the court what he said was a part-nership agreement between Owen Pearce and himself. The agreement was drafted in Wingate's hand and pur-ports to bear the signature of each party. Its terms are contrary to logic and, if genuine, reflect unsound busi-ness judgment on the part of Owen Pearce to Wingate's advantage. Here again, the judge accepted Wingate's position on the matter."

Ellsworth stood up from his chair.

"I think it is time that I visit Geoffrey Wingate."

Then, to my surprise, he added, "I would like you

to come with me. Your presence joined with mine will unsettle him. And I can benefit from your transcription skills."

I answered without fully considering the implications inherent in what was involved.

"When would we go?"

"Now."

Twenty minutes later, we were in a hackney carriage on the way to Wingate's home. The timing of Ellsworth's offer had left me no time to reflect upon the risk to my person that I was likely to incur. Now I was in an uneasy state of mind. Two men were presumed to have died at Wingate's hand. I pushed that thought aside.

The ride continued. I asked myself if Amanda would be at home. That led to the realisation that it was incumbent upon me to tell Ellsworth about escorting her to the ballet.

"Is there anything more that I should know?" the inspector asked when I was done.

"That is all."

As we approached Wingate's residence, Ellsworth offered a final thought on the matter at hand.

"A man who commits murder will confront its aftermath with effrontery. If it weighed on his conscience—if he had a conscience at all—he would not have committed the crime. But there are degrees of hardness in the hardest metal and shades of colour in black itself. He can be broken."

The inspector turned to face me.

"You are to transcribe all that is said once the interview begins and remain silent to the greatest extent possible. I expect you to heed these instructions."

We arrived unannounced at Wingate's residence. Ellsworth hit the brass knocker against the door, and a servant answered.

"Is Mr. Wingate at home?" the inspector queried.

The servant recognised me from previous visits. But it was Ellworth who had addressed him, and he responded to Ellsworth.

"Who should I say is calling, sir?"

"Inspector Benjamin Ellsworth of the Metropolitan Police Force."

The servant left us and returned several minutes later.

"Come with me, please."

Amanda was not in sight as we walked through the house. Wingate was sitting behind his desk when we entered his office. It took a moment for him to consider the implications inherent in Ellsworth and I being together. He was adding up the weights and measures in his mind when the inspector spoke.

"Geoffrey Wingate?"

"I am."

"I am Inspector Benjamin Ellsworth of the Metropolitan Police Force. I believe that you are familiar with Mr. Dickens."

"I did not know that police inspectors travel with newspaper boys."

"Mr. Dickens is assisting me. His shorthand skills are of great value."

There was an outward calm on Wingate's face, though a bit more colour in it than I had seen before. He understood at that point that the inspector and I were united. Whatever either of us knew separately, it was likely to be worse for him now that our knowledge was joined.

Ellsworth sat uninvited in a chair. I followed his lead and took a transcription pad from my coat pocket.

Wingate leaned back in his chair, settled into a position of repose, and looked at the inspector with an expression that seemed to say, "This is an amusing fellow. I will hear him out." Then he yawned.

Ellsworth began. "It is my duty, sir, in the position which I hold, to inform you that—"

"I'm a busy man," Wingate interrupted with the air of one who, by reason of his superior place in society, has the right to speak condescendingly to another. "My time is precious even if yours is not. Come to the point, and I will imagine all that ought to have been said before."

"I speak to you from the heart—"

"Don't be absurd," Wingate interrupted again. "The heart is the center of the blood vessels, an ingenious part of our formation. Men are some times stabbed in the heart or shot in the heart. But as to speaking from the heart or being warm-hearted or cold-hearted or broken-hearted, those things are nonsense. The heart has no more to do with what you say or think than your knees have."

"I am not as clever as you are," Ellsworth continued. "But the truth raises me to your level. Let me ask you first about Owen Pearce."

"He had the misfortune to die, as all of us shall some day."

"But he died rather young. And I find it curious that you are in possession of so much that belonged once to another man."

"The legal papers were in proper order. I conducted no business that was not to the full satisfaction of the court. I find your questions rather dull."

"Blunt tools are some times of use where sharper instruments fail."

"And you misjudge the limits of my patience."

"Your patience is not my concern. Let me be plain with you and play a fairer game than when you held all the cards and Owen Pearce saw only the backs."

Wingate glared with eyes as cutting as swords. "You fail to understand who I am," he said with an air of patronage.

"To the contrary, Mr. Wingate. You are no stranger to me. I understand your kind well."

"And you have no idea of what went on in Owen Pearce's home. Perhaps you have spoken with Lenora Pearce. I am sure she did not tell you that she had a lover."

Ellsworth sat silent.

Wingate smiled a dark wicked smile.

"That is correct, sir. A lover. At times, I have wondered whether Lenora was not complicit in Owen's murder. He loved her and confided in me that he was hurt terribly by her conduct. It was the reason he changed several financial instruments in the months before his death."

"The instruments are fraudulent," Ellsworth said calmly. "Through procedures of detection developed only recently at Scotland Yard, we have determined that a forgery was committed. And there is more. We have found a witness who saw Owen Pearce and another man walking together and then heard a gunshot moments before the body was found."

Wingate started when Ellsworth spoke those words. It was a slight start, quickly repressed and checked. But he did start, though he made it a part of taking a handkerchief out of his pocket and blowing his nose.

"The witness will identify you as that man who was walking with Owen Pearce."

"My dear Mr. Ellsworth. Have you really lived to your present age and remained so simple as to approach a gentleman of my established character and credentials with nonsense such as this?"

"The sordid tale is all there, capable of being proven by the prosecution in a court of law."

"It is not possible for you to prove blame upon me. The law of England supposes every man to be innocent until he is proved—proved—to be guilty. Either you know that, or you do not. Which is it?"

Ellsworth stared hard into Wingate's eyes. There was silence between them, but I detected a twitching at Wingate's mouth and perhaps an involuntary attraction of his right hand in the direction of the inspector's cravat.

"Did you speak to me, sir?" Ellsworth queried.

"I did not."

"Perhaps you wished to speak."

"I did not do that either."

"Very well then. Let us move to the subject of Florence Spriggs."

A look of fear crossed Wingate's eyes, quickly replaced by defiance and contempt.

"What of Miss Spriggs?" he demanded.

"Did you know her?"

"She was my companion at one time. I am sorry to say that she proved treacherous and ungrateful."

"And James Frost?"

"He was of the streets, and he died on the streets. What more is there to be said?"

"One might speak of the manner in which he died."

Wingate's eyes turned cold and calculating. His face was stern, but his colour was changing, and he seemed to breathe as if he had been running.

"Speak to the walls of my office, sir," he said angrily, rising from his chair. "I will listen to no more of this. Speak also to my desk. They are attentive listeners and will not interrupt you. Make this room yours, and I will return when you have finished what you have to say."

"Sit down," Ellsworth ordered.

Wingate stood still with his hand on the back of his chair. He tried to stand scornfully, but it appeared as though he needed the chair for support. He fixed his eyes on a silver pencil case on the desk, as a tightrope walker on a dangerous wire might keep an object in his sight to steady himself lest he lose his balance and fall.

Then he sat, a scowl of hatred on his face.

"Do your duty, Mr. Ellsworth. But be careful not to overstep it. If you exceed your authority, I have friends in high places who will be displeased."

"You are a low, murderous, mercenary villain, and it shall be proven by the evidence against you in a court of law."

"I am not sure I heard you correctly," Wingate said, summoning up one last effort to establish control over his antagonist. "Could you repeat what you just said."

Ellsworth met Wingate's icy stare with one of his own. Then he turned in my direction and nodded toward my transcription pad. "Mr. Dickens?"

For the first time since we sat down in the office, I spoke.

"You are a low, murderous, mercenary villain, and it shall be proven by the evidence against you in a court of law."

Wingate stared at Ellsworth as a reptile might when looking for a hole to hide in. A stoppage came upon his breathing. His nostrils rose and fell convulsively, but I saw no moving at his mouth. His figure appeared to shrink.

"Have you ever seen a public hanging?" Ellsworth asked.

There was no response.

Now Ellsworth was wielding his voice as a weapon in the same manner as Wingate had before.

"You think you are a superior breed of man, but death and fire make equals of us all. You shall see me again in court when you are tried for your life. The charge will be willful murder, twice done. That, and your assault on Miss Spriggs."

Wingate raised a fist above his head and slammed it down upon his desk with the force of a blacksmith.

"That whore you would make an angel of! That low girl I picked out of the mud!"

"You shall know her worth and that of James Frost when the hangman's noose is placed round your neck. The boards will spring open, and you will fall as dead weight. There will be a sudden jerk, a convulsion of the limbs, and you will hang there, swinging lifeless before the cheering mob."

"A curse upon you," Wingate shrieked.

"The curse may pass your lips, but it is empty breath.

You have no greater power to call a curse down upon me than you have to make a drop of rain fall from the sky. The rope for your necklace is being woven as we speak. It would be my pleasure to place it round your neck, but that privilege shall fall to other hands."

Wingate looked now as though the ground beneath him was sliding away.

"I will be here again soon," the inspector pledged. "It is a beautiful case, and I expect to supply what little is left to complete it within a few days. You shall be taken into custody on a warrant shortly." Ellsworth rose from his chair. "Our meeting is over, sir."

"London is large," Wingate said weakly. "We can easily find different ways. Please, show me which way is yours. I will take another and make it worth your while."

"I assure you, Mr. Wingate, whatever road you take, our paths will cross again. You have lost the game, and you will pay for your sins."

I followed Ellsworth's lead to the door. Then, from behind, I heard Wingate's voice, possessed of more firmness than a moment before.

"Mr. Dickens. I have tried to befriend you. But our lives lie in very different directions now."

I did not answer. I knew that Ellsworth preferred it that way.

"I had a dream about you last night, Mr. Dickens. It was quite unpleasant. I thrust an ice pick into your heart."

The inspector turned to face him. "Rest assured, Mr. Wingate," he said with calm in his voice, "others in positions of power know what Mr. Dickens and I know.

If harm were to befall either one of us, it would do you no good. It would simply add to the ledger against you."

❦

Ellsworth sat silent in the carriage as we rode away from Wingate's home. He seemed to be pondering the day's events, and I thought it unwise to distract him.

Finally, he spoke.

"If Wingate could kill us with a wish, we would not live long."

I am certain that I looked unsettled by those words.

"I am not unmindful of your safety," the inspector added. "Do not leave your home tonight. Tomorrow morning, a constable will be assigned to accompany you whenever you are away from your quarters. He will be at your residence each day at the hour you specify and will escort you home when your work is done."

Ellsworth paused to gather his thoughts.

"Wingate was not penitent in the least this afternoon. There is no more contrition or remorse in him now than there was when the evil deeds were done. Every man and woman should have their rights and their punishment according to justice while they are still here on this earth. I hope that is achieved here."

"You have witnesses now."

Ellsworth shook his head.

"There was a great amount of a bluff in what I said. We have little that would hold against him in a court of law. There is no proof of forgery and no witness to the murder of Owen Pearce. But Wingate does not know that. And he is desperate. Only a desperate man or a fool would talk the way he did today. And he is not a fool."

Then Ellsworth did something that I had never seen him do before. He smiled.

"Truth is a sublime and grand thing," he said. "Though like other sublime and grand things, such as a thunderstorm, one is not always glad to see it. I believe he is crumbling. Let us see if it leads him to error."

CHAPTER 9

My recollection turns a corner now to a day in my life like no other. If it had occurred yesterday, I could not remember the details more clearly. Every moment is firmly impressed upon my memory, as if it had been carved in stone and set before my eyes since birth. It is a secret that I have held inviolate for four and thirty years.

On Tuesday, the twenty-ninth day of March, the morning after Benjamin Ellsworth conducted his interview with Geoffrey Wingate, a police constable named Clarence Evans met me at my lodging. He stayed with me throughout the day as I travelled through London and brought me home safely that night. I told him that there would be no need for his services on Wednesday. The first installment of *The Pickwick Papers* was to be published on Thursday. I would be at home all day on Wednesday, working to complete the second installment.

Wednesday morning was of a kind that is common in early spring when the year is fickle and changeable in its youth. The sun shone hot, and the wind blew cold. It was spring in the light and winter in the shade.

I awoke early and began to write. Geoffrey Wingate was very much on my mind, but I pushed the thought of him aside as best I could to concentrate on my work. Catherine and I were to be married on Saturday. I felt an uneasiness with regard to the impending nuptials.

I finished the second installment in the late afternoon and read through what I had written, moving sentences, changing a word here and there. Samuel Pickwick and Alfred Jingle were coming alive. Then I heard tapping at my door.

A knock, louder.

I went to the door.

"Who is there?"

"Amanda Wingate."

It is in the character of young men that, when the prize is sufficient, caution with regard to mortality is some times cast aside.

I opened the door. Amanda Wingate stood before me. Her attire was drab and plain. A black coat and gray dress without much shape to it. Her skirt extended to within inches of the floor. She held a large cloth bag in her hand.

"I have come to share a bottle of wine with you, Mr. Dickens. As a mark of our friendship."

Her eyes promised that she intended no harm. I chose to believe them.

"You surprise me, Mrs. Wingate. And more so because you are here alone."

"I am a grown woman, Mr. Dickens. I go when and where I please."

She stepped into my rooms and removed her bonnet. Her hair was tied atop her head in a bun.

"It is spring," she said cheerfully. "The trees are budding."

I do not recall precisely what I offered in response. Perhaps that summer was likely to follow.

Amanda handed me a green glass bottle.

"Have you glasses for wine? I brought a corkscrew on the chance that you do not have one."

I took two glasses from the cupboard and set them on the table. Amanda handed the corkscrew to me. I opened the bottle and filled each glass with wine. We sat opposite each other.

Poison . . . The thought was inevitable.

"You are not drinking, Mr. Dickens. Is the wine not to your liking?"

"I find it sad to drink alone."

Amanda raised her glass to her lips and swallowed all that was in it. A trickle of red coursed down her chin. She wiped her mouth on the sleeve of her dress and gestured for me to pour more.

I refilled her glass.

She looked around the room. "I like it that you have books, Mr. Dickens. I read books."

"What have you read?"

"*Waverley, Gulliver's Travels, The Fortunes and Misfortunes of Moll Flanders.*"

The light of the late afternoon sun was dancing on the wall. I did not know why she had come. I knew only that she was there.

"Do you think 'Amanda' is a pretty name, Mr. Dickens?"

"I like it."

"It is of Latin origin and means 'worthy of love.'"

I would play the game no more.

"Have you come to see me about Geoffrey?"

"Geoffrey does not know that I am here."

"But your appearance is connected to events of this week, is it not?"

"I know that Geoffrey has been agitated. Perhaps you can tell me why."

"His integrity and conduct have been called into question."

"I choose not to believe that about him."

"You are extremely lenient in your appraisal."

"I know what it is like to be the object of uncharitable suspicions. And he is my husband."

"Do you fear him?"

"Of course not."

"You should."

Her eyes flashed angrily.

"I will not hear of such things."

"Do you fear what you might hear?"

"Talk of Geoffrey is not why I came."

"Why did you come?"

Her eyes changed.

"I wanted to see you."

There were no words within me to respond.

Amanda reached above her head and pulled the ribbon from her hair. Her long brown tresses fell loose round her shoulders.

"Do you think me a wicked woman?"

"My mind is at a loss for thoughts at the moment."

"It is in my nature."

There are moral ambiguities in life. I was not thinking of them.

Amanda reached again, this time behind her shoulders, and unfastened the buttons that held her dress together. The customary petticoats were not beneath it. What little she now wore was striking for its colour. It was the fashion of the time for cloth that touched the most private parts of a woman's body to be white in keeping with the purity of the wearer. Amanda's most intimate undergarments were black and fashioned to accentuate rather than conceal.

She stood now virtually naked before me. I could have looked at her forever.

"This must be known only to us," she said.

She took my hand and pressed it against her broad white bosom. I had no more chance of resisting her than of standing on the shore of the ocean and pushing back the tide. Whether our lips came together next on her movement or mine matters little. It happened. Then she drew back, just a bit.

"Have you experience?"

"This is the first time," I confessed. "I am young for my age in matters of this nature."

"I prefer it that way. We are both clean. Come to the bed with me. We haven't much time."

She led me by the hand to my bedroom and passed her fingers along my cheek. They trembled for just a moment before their touch became a caress. She was a hundred times more beautiful unclothed than I had imagined anyone could be. I have never seen a woman as beautiful as she was that night.

"Do I please you, Mr. Dickens?"

It is happening now. Amanda is at arm's length. The length of an arm is not much. And she is not holding it out straight but bending it a little. There is a smile on her face. She is coming closer. Her hair covers my face like an angel's wing. The room and walls grow dim. I am in a misty, unsettled state. The rest is like a dream. She is passion. She is fire. She is the essence of desire, more than human to me. She is everything that I can ever want. She understands my every need. The heavens open up and rain pleasure down upon me. It is too late to part us. There is a torrent of ecstasy. I am swallowed up in an abyss of love. Then, exhaustion.

If I had left the world in that moment, it would have been on happier terms than I have known before or since in my life.

Amanda lay beside me, her hair disheveled, her bosom heaving. I kissed her cheek. Her eyes were dim with moisture that might have been taken for tears. She rested her head upon my chest as though she had known me from the cradle. Then she spoke.

"I must go now," she said.

"Please, stay longer."

"I cannot."

Amanda rose from the bed. The room was dark. I lit a candle. She began putting on her clothes. A contented laugh escaped her lips, childlike with a touch of wickedness.

A sentiment was growing powerfully within me, ever more difficult to suppress.

"Must you be with Geoffrey?"

I thought the question but did not ask it. There was nothing to be gained by that line of inquiry.

"You are thinking something," Amanda said. "I see it in your face."

I nodded.

"A penny for your thoughts."

"I was thinking that perhaps I expect more of you than you expect of yourself."

Her eyes flashed angrily, as I had seen before when I ventured too far.

"Don't talk nonsense."

"It is intended as a compliment."

"Then keep your compliments to yourself. You have no idea what I expect of myself, and you have no right to judge me. You are not a stupid man, Mr. Dickens. You have an idea of what I once did. But you have no idea of what my life was like when I was young, or what I am today."

"Perhaps I know more than you think."

"Not at all. You are a clever man, but you are quite young in knowledge of human nature. Let me tell you of the world I grew up in since you are so curious about it all.

"There was a child called Amanda, born into poverty and neglect. A child who had done no wrong but to come into the world alive. She knew no father. She did not know where she had been born. She first became aware of herself at the age of four, living on the streets of

London. She had a mother who did not care for her. She had no schooling. She was taught nothing of religion. Nobody kept watch over her to protect her. Nobody! The only care she knew was to be beaten and abused. She did not lose her innocence. She never had any.

"You have seen children, Mr. Dickens. Half-naked shivering figures that gaze with hungry eyes at the loaves of bread in shop windows. The thin sheet of glass that their pale faces press against is a wall of iron to them. I was one of those children.

"I had a brother who disappeared on the streets one day when he was seven. He was never seen or heard from again. My brother! Gone forever. That is the world I come from.

"When I was young, I was skin and bones. As womanhood came upon me and my body changed, my mother made a property of me. I was groomed for trade and sold to men who took me for their pleasure. I became pregnant. My mother brought me to a doctor of sorts, and they killed the baby before it could grow in my womb. The procedure changed what is inside me. I can never be with child again. Do you know how old I was then, Mr. Dickens? I was twelve. Make no judgment of me.

"I brought good looks out of childhood. Virtue as you think of it was a luxury that I could not afford. What came next comes to many women. I took advantage of the opportunities that my appearance afforded me. I suffered myself to be sold as ignominiously as any beast with a halter round its neck. I was offered and accepted, put up and appraised, until my soul sickened. Every grace that was a resource to me was paraded and vended to enhance my value. Somehow, I came through it all without disease. I resolved that I would be well cared for and looked after. I became educated.

"I am a woman now, honoured by society. There is talk, I am sure, among the wives when I am not there. But I treat people of all classes with dignity and respect, as they now treat me. Perhaps you think I would have been better served had I taken up maid's work or sewn clothes or scrubbed streets to earn my roll of bread from day to day. I think not. Let all who would save my soul ask themselves where they were when I was an innocent, helpless little wretch. Let them understand that there is twenty times more wickedness and wrong among the rich than on the streets where I once lived. Why should I be penitent, and those born to wealth go free?"

Having spoken those words, Amanda lapsed into silence. Her face, which had been agitated, softened.

"I am done," she said. "I have said enough. Let us not talk of honourable living. Perhaps, in some small way, your childhood was like mine. We need not make a show of our history. It was over long ago."

Her beauty, fierce and defiant moments before, was now gentle in spirit.

I could no longer suppress the question.

"Do you love Geoffrey?"

"There was a time when I thought I did."

"Does he love you?"

"He has been good to me in his way."

"You could have chosen a more honourable man."

"Don't talk to me of honour, Mr. Dickens. I dined with the woman who you are planning to marry. The daughter of your employer. A step up in society from where you began. That consideration, I am sure, was not lost on you when you proposed marriage. Or is it chance that you are not engaged to a woman who began her life on the streets?"

The words I spoke next came without thought.

"I would leave her for you."

"Don't talk rubbish. Leave her for me. I am a married woman, thank you, with no interest in leaving my husband. And you have no intention of deviating from the path that you have chosen for yourself. You are an ambitious man. I see that in you. You are as driven in your way as Geoffrey is in his. I do not think that scandal would suit you."

The candle was burning low. Amanda was now fully dressed and looked as proper as when she had arrived, save for a smudge of wine on her sleeve.

"I know what I am," she said. "I know the rules of society. Some times I abide by them. Some times I do not. I know the difference between right and wrong. I have done both in my life. As for the life I lead, I must lead it."

"Why did you do this tonight?"

"Because I wanted to, Mr. Dickens. What other reason could there be? I chose to be with you this evening as I chose to go with you to the ballet. The difference is that, tonight, Geoffrey does not know that I am here. I trust you agree that it would be unwise to tell him."

"I do."

"Then we are of the same mind. One keeps a secret better than two. You must keep this one with me."

"The secret is yours, not mine. I promise that I will respect it."

"Then there is only one thing more that I would ask of you."

Amanda reached into the bag that she had brought with her and drew out a book bound in dark green cloth. I recognised it immediately. Volume I from the first series of *Sketches by Boz*.

"Would you be so kind as to inscribe this for me?"

I carried the book to my desk and opened it to the title page. Amanda was smiling, but it seemed a smile that could easily turn to tears. I reached for my pen and wrote:

> *For Amanda Wingate,*
> *a woman of uncommon beauty and grace.*
> *My fondest good wishes,*
> *Charles Dickens*

"Thank you, Mr. Dickens. I will treasure this always."

"It is my pleasure."

"We are parting now. I shall not see you again."

My heart, which minutes before had been soaring, sank suddenly like a stone.

"But surely—"

"Never again. It must be that way." Her voice softened. "But let us part as friends."

She extended her hand. I put it to my lips and kissed it.

"It is dark out," I pled. "Let me accompany you home."

"There is no need for that. I will be safe. I know my way about the streets."

❦

The hours after Amanda's departure were tumultuous in my mind. I did not realise then that she would be forever fixed in my consciousness. I did know that my life had changed. I also knew that I had hoped from the beginning that what had just transpired would come to pass. But I had never for a moment thought that it would happen. I felt no guilt or shame at having betrayed Catherine. There was a modicum of fear for my personal safety, but I sensed that Amanda would protect me.

On my bed, I found a handkerchief. Silk with two violets embroidered into the cloth. I wondered if Amanda had left it by design. I vowed to keep it forever.

That night, I dreamed of her, as I often would in the years to come.

The first installment of *The Pickwick Papers* was published the following morning. Clarence Evans met me at my rooms and escorted me throughout the day. Amanda was dominant in my thoughts. My fantasies ran wild. Geoffrey Wingate would be prosecuted and sent to the gallows. Amanda would be disgraced in the eyes of some. No matter. She understood my cause. She was born of it. Would that I could read the book of her heart. I knew little of it other than I longed for it to be mine.

On Friday morning, Clarence Evans returned to my quarters. Forty hours had passed since Amanda and I had parted.

"Inspector Ellsworth wishes to see you at the Wingate residence," Evans told me. "He would like you to transcribe the statements of witnesses as he speaks with them."

The constable was without further knowledge to answer my questions. Had Wingate crumbled and confessed guilt? Had Amanda known more than she acknowledged to me and resolved to tell all? The carriage ride to the Wingate home seemed to last forever. My heart was pounding.

Several more constables were in the parlour with the servant staff when I arrived. I was led to Wingate's office. Ellsworth looked up from behind the desk and addressed me as I entered.

"They are gone."

It took a moment for me to grasp the meaning of those simple words.

"Last night, under cover of dark, they fled," the inspector said.

Files had been pulled from cabinets. The charred remains of what had once been Wingate's account ledgers lay on the floor in a corner of the room. The large painting of a naval engagement hanging opposite the window caught my eye. I looked at it more closely than I had before.

Burning hulls, bursting magazines; great guns exploding and tearing men to pieces; drowning sailors clinging to unseaworthy spars as others floated dead.

"The captain has deserted his ship," Ellsworth said. "Come, let us look around."

Room by room, I followed him through the house. The Wingates had taken whatever they could in direct proportion of monetary value to size. Jewel cases were empty and drawers flung open, as though thieves had entered in the middle of the night.

All of Amanda's jewelry was gone. Her many gowns and the mirrors that had reflected her beauty when they adorned her had a desolate air. We passed the harp in the sitting room off the parlour where I had first seen her. In due course, Ellsworth brought the servant staff before me, and I transcribed what was said.

A chronology emerged. Wingate was extremely upset on Monday afternoon after the inspector and I sat with him. On Tuesday, his condition was the same. There was a flurry of activity on Wednesday and Thursday, with Wingate leaving the house several times, possibly to visit banks.

Amanda had come to my quarters late Wednesday afternoon. Had she known of their impending flight?

"We are parting now," she had told me. "I shall not see you again."

On Thursday night, they fled.

Amanda's lady's maid, Clarice, was the last of the servant staff to be questioned. She was clearly distraught. Clarice described how Amanda had shaken hands with each of the servants before departing and had turned for one last look at the house.

"She was dressed very plainly," Clarice recalled. "And her hair was hidden under a shawl. All her fine clothes were left behind. That must have broke her heart."

"What was Mrs. Wingate like?" I queried.

Ellsworth did not object to my question although, clearly, it overstepped my role.

"Very kind," Clarice answered. "Mr. Wingate spoke harshly to us at times. Mrs. Wingate never said a word but was pleasant and right. She was a lady, and we were common people, but she talked with us as though we were of her own station in life."

She stopped, as though wrestling with the propriety of what she was to say next.

"Go on," I urged.

"Mrs. Wingate swore us to secrecy. But before she left—God bless her heart—she gave each of us fifty pounds. She warned us that Mr. Wingate would be angry with her if he knew. He spoke cruelly to her at times. She tried so hard to be a dutiful wife. How brave and strong her heart. She was crying when they left. And she said to me, 'He is trampled down and ruined. I have an obligation as his wife. I cannot leave him now.'"

"A graceful woman," Ellsworth noted. "Capable of doing honour to Wingate's name and reflecting credit on his proprietorship. Quite ornamental, too, no doubt."

When the interviews were done, I sat with the inspector in the parlour.

"Do you suppose he has much money with him?" I asked.

"I should think that he has pocketed a good amount in one way or another," Ellsworth answered. "The total of what has been left behind for his investors will be expressed in arithmetic by a circle. But the money he has will soon be gone. And whatever object he pursues after that, he will do so crookedly."

"Will you find him?"

"The world is a large place. To search for him would be hopeless. We will leave his discovery to time and chance and to Heaven's pleasure."

"Then he goes free."

Ellsworth shook his head.

"We are well to be rid of him. I am a practical man, Mr. Dickens. His flight confirms his guilt. And he is being punished more than the law would have allowed.

Despite what we know in our hearts, the proof to convict him in a court of law is not there. He has left behind most of what he owned. What the world thinks of him now and how it looks at him will be the haunting demon of his mind. He will imagine pursuers in every place. He will see them pointing at him in the street, seeking him out among the crowd, and whispering behind wherever he goes. He will hear their footsteps outside his window when he is shut up in his room in bed at night. He will be restless everywhere. Under the circumstances, that is the best punishment we could have hoped for."

"And that is all?"

"I know his kind. He will not do well."

Book 3

CHAPTER 10

On Saturday, the second of April, two days after Geoffrey and Amanda Wingate fled from London, I married Catherine Hogarth. The ceremony took place in Saint Luke's Church. I understood more fully by then that my romance of Catherine was a love born of ambition more than the heart. But it was too late to turn back.

We lay together for the first time in the wedding bed that night. Catherine giggled. She squealed. I knew that I had erred horribly. I closed my eyes and imagined myself with another as the dungeon door of marriage slammed shut upon my life. I would never be free.

Toward the end of April, I returned to the Wingate home with Benjamin Ellsworth for one last look about. Well-muscled men were moving heavy furnishings, while two gentlemen with pens made out inventories in preparation for auction. Workers sat upon pieces of furniture never made to be sat upon and ate bread and cheese off other pieces of furniture never made to be eaten from. Chaotic combinations of belongings appeared. Mattresses and bedding in the dining room; glass and china in the conservatory; the great dinner service in heaps on the divan in the parlour.

Wingate's flight had loosened tongues. The nature of his business was now clear. Investors had given him money to invest in various financial undertakings. By contract, he was allowed to retain a modest percentage of each investment as his commission. In practice, he had invested only a small portion of the money that was entrusted to him and appropriated the rest for his own personal use.

Men who should have known better—some honest, some not—deferred to his every word. They fawned and flattered and smiled as he showed them neatly kept balance sheets that detailed the manner in which he had turned their ten thousand pounds into twenty thousand.

The nature of the supposed investments allowed for the fraud. The entirety of the principle for an annuity comes in at the beginning and then dribbles back in small payments to the holder. The premiums for life assurance policies that Wingate purported to purchase were paid in advance. If the holder of a policy died, premiums paid to purchase fictitious policies for other holders covered the death benefits. Investors were told that their money was invested in the stock of various companies. They received dividends regularly and were assured that their principle was growing. In fact, there was no principle. It was imaginary wealth. Fraud concealed more fraud. Through it all, Wingate spent lavishly to maintain his luxurious way of life. By the time he fled, there was little for him to liquidate and take with him.

"It is remarkable," Ellsworth told me. "People gave their money to Wingate to invest, and they knew no more about him than they might know about a man they met at the tailor shop. Men have such extraordinary powers of persuasion when exerted over themselves. The next criminal in delicate disguise who is comfortable living outside the law for the purpose of swindling will succeed as well."

Two days later, the pulpit of the auctioneer was erected. Something within me compelled my return for the auction. Herds of vampires were overrunning rooms, sounding glasses with their knuckles, striking discordant notes on the harp, balancing the silver spoons and forks, punching the cushions of chairs and sofas with their dirty fists, opening and shutting all the drawers, examining the threads of the drapery and linen. A vile-looking woman with a screeching voice won the bid on the lavender silk gown that Amanda had worn on the evening that I went with her to the ballet. There was not a secret place in the whole house.

It would have been just if Florence Spriggs and Lenora Pearce had been allowed to claim a portion of the gain from the sale of the house and its contents. But wealthy investors who suffered losses in Wingate's scheme had already staked their claim.

All day long, there was a retinue of moving carts in the street outside the residence. Then it was over. Nothing was left. As I rode home that night, I asked myself how much Amanda had known of her husband's ways. I asked, as I would do a thousand times in later years, why she had taken me to bed. It was folly to think that I was the only man she had seduced in that manner. And yet . . .

The road she had chosen lay before her. She would follow it with her own self-willed step, and I would travel mine. I did not know where she was, only that there was an immeasurable distance between us and an empty place in my heart.

❦

Catherine soon became pregnant, and we moved to a house at 48 Doughty Street. It was significantly larger than my previous rooms and reflected optimism with regard to my financial future.

There was a print run of one thousand copies of the first installment of *The Pickwick Papers*. Disappointing sales led to a smaller printing of the next three installments. Then the character of Sam Weller—Samuel Pickwick's valet—was introduced, and sales soared. Forty thousand copies of the twentieth and final installment were printed.

The success of *Pickwick* gave me my first taste of renown. It had been publicly acknowledged in a publisher's advertisement that "Boz" was in fact Charles Dickens. I was keenly alive to the praise that sounded in my ears. Then I took what was perhaps the most important step upon my journey to becoming an author.

It was a time in England when eighteenth-century customs with regard to labour, schools, orphanages, and democracy itself were being reevaluated. The Poor

Law Amendment Act of 1834 had replaced a system of parish-by-parish measures intended to deal with the problems of the poor. Or rather, the problems posed by the poor. It called for a centralised system of workhouses to be built, with no person receiving assistance from the state unless he or she lived in one. The poorhouses were kept in abominable and scandalous condition. Separate institutions were maintained for children, able-bodied men, able-bodied women, and the old. Families were torn apart. Mothers were separated from their children. Wages were less than those paid to the poorest free labourer.

I wanted to speak to the poor houses and to what it is like to live at the lowest levels of society. I did so through the eyes of a child: Oliver Twist.

Oliver stood for countless children born and bred in neglect. They have never known what childhood is, never been taught to love a parent's smile or to dread a parent's frown. The gaiety and innocence of childhood are unknown to them. Talk to them of parental solicitude and the merry games of infancy, and they will stare at you with unknowing eyes. Tell them of hunger and beggary and the streets, and they will understand.

They sleep at night packed close together, covered only by their ragged clothes. There are some who, lying on their backs with upturned faces, bear more the aspect of dead bodies than of living creatures. A few among the youngest of the children sleep peacefully with smiles upon their faces. As morning takes the place of night, their smiles fade away.

I wrote *Oliver Twist* with greater power than I had been able to summon up before. Friends told me that publishing in installments was a low form of commerce and that, by continuing in that form, I would encumber my future. I resisted their warnings and did as I would do with my writing throughout my life.

Oliver Twist spoke directly to the people. It portrayed the innate goodness and suffering of common men and women, the random nature of death, and the triumph of good over evil. Its serialisation made it accessible to all. Men and women gathered together with the publication of each installment, combined their resources for the one-shilling purchase price, and searched for one who could read aloud to the others.

The bond between my readers and myself was now a personal attachment. I was aware that my work was capable of stirring feeling among the downtrodden and also of influencing the debate among the powerful on matters of importance.

Whoever is devoted to an art must deliver himself wholly up to it. Ambition and hard work were the keys to my success. As a rule, I woke at seven o'clock each morning, took a cold shower, ate breakfast, and wrote from nine until three in the afternoon. On some days, I ate a modest lunch at my desk. I wrote with a goose quill pen and blue ink an average of two thousand words each day. After writing, I walked for several hours, dined at six, and retired by midnight.

When I wrote, my work had complete possession of my thoughts. My creations spoke to me. When I sat with pen and paper, reality and imagination were so blended that it was impossible to separate them in my mind. A voice kept whispering to me: greatness.

I wrote with speed. *The Life and Adventures of Nicholas Nickleby, The Old Curiosity Shop, Barnaby Rudge.* I became a businessman as well as an author to ensure that I was fairly paid. When I was a child, the family had endured frequent moves as a matter of necessity as my father sought to evade his creditors. Now we moved by choice to an even larger house near Regent's Park at 1 Devonshire Street.

It was rare for an author to live off the sale of his work without family funds or a benefactor to support him. By my thirtieth birthday, my earnings easily covered the expenses of what was becoming a rather large family. My clothes were more costly than before, and I was acquiring things of material value to have in the home.

It was during this time, when royalties from the sale of my work had become substantial, that I committed myself to one particular act of charity. I resolved to give a stipend to Florence Spriggs and pay for the schooling of her daughter Ruby. I found my way to the place where they had lived, but the hovel was no longer there. It had been torn down, or, more likely, it had fallen of its own state. No one could tell me where they had gone or whether they were alive or dead.

I sought out Benjamin Ellsworth, who by then had risen to the rank of district superintendent, and asked for his assistance.

"Leave it alone," Ellsworth cautioned. "The probabilities are such that you do not want to know their fate."

I did not pursue the truth. I feared what I might find.

On the fourth of January, 1842, I embarked upon a new adventure, a journey to America. I arrived in Boston after eighteen days at sea and was now in the Land of Liberty, although any land would have satisfied me after so much water.

My reputation had preceded me, and my presence was very much in demand. So many people of note sought to speak with me that the British Consulate arranged for a daily reception at Tremont House in Boston, where I was lodged.

I had come to America to meet a new people, see nature at its most beautiful, and gather insights for a book. After my stay in Boston, I journeyed to New York, where three thousand people attended The Great Boz Ball at the Park Theatre in my honour. Then I visited a dozen more cities and Niagara Falls, where I was moved by Nature's splendour.

There were elegant parties, formal dinners, and meetings with Henry Wadsworth Longfellow, Washington Irving, and Edgar Allan Poe. In the capital of America, I was introduced to John Quincy Adams, Daniel Webster, Henry Clay, and John Tyler, President of the United States.

But America was not the republic that I had imagined. The factory system and treatment of labour were more enlightened than in England. However, there was a negative side to the ledger.

There was no respect for copyright in America. Pirate editions of my work were widely sold without any payment to me. Whenever protection of copyright was discussed, it was opposed on the ground that literature and knowledge should belong to The People.

Worse, I had no privacy in America. Crowds gathered whenever I appeared in public. If I walked down the street, I was followed by a multitude. If I went to the theatre, people stared at me as though I were a marble statue to be commented upon. If I dined out, I had to talk to everybody about everything. If I stayed at the hotel, it became like a fair with callers. If I went to a party, I was so enclosed and hemmed about that I was exhausted for want of air. I could not drink a glass of water without a dozen people looking down my throat when I opened my mouth to swallow. There was no time for rest or peace. I wearied of giving myself up to spectacle as though I were public property.

I was handed newspaper accounts of discussions as to whether I was shorter than people had expected or taller or thinner or fatter or younger or older; whether my eyes were brown or blue or hazel or green; whether my attire was flashy or tasteful, gentlemanly or vulgar.

I will admit to being a bit vain in matters of appearance. For most of my life, I have been partial to theatrical dress. Dinner jackets with velvet and satin trim, brightly coloured waistcoats, noticeable jewelry. That said, it did my mood no good to pick up a newspaper and read that I was foppish, inclined toward dandyism, and very English in appearance although not the best English. And concern for my crude, vulgar, flamboyant behaviour did not keep the barber who cut my hair from sweeping up the locks and selling them to the public.

After six months, I returned home from America and docked in Liverpool. The writing of *American Notes* followed. In my previous writing, I had never shown any disposition to soften my commentary on what is ridiculous or wrong in England. I had assumed that the people who had honoured me so extravagantly in America would be indisposed to quarrel were I to apply the same standard to their own country. I was wrong. Nonetheless, my time in America endowed me with greater understanding of my fame and the power that my literary creations placed at my command.

With the publication of *A Christmas Carol* and *The Life and Adventures of Martin Chuzzlewit,* my career grew even more prosperous. I was caressed by the public and courted by the rich and powerful. Common men and women loved my work because it was about them. Members of the aristocracy welcomed me into their homes as the famous Charles Dickens. I had completed the journey from humble origins to recognition as a gentleman and was a guest of distinction at any gathering. People responded in haste to my requests, and my requests became demands.

I continued to advocate for causes that I believed in. *Dombey and Son* and *The Personal History and Experience of David Copperfield* flowed from my pen.

As my fortune grew, my father was creative in finding ways to borrow against my credit. He had never become a responsible provider. At times, he went so far as to forge my name as the guarantor of his debts. He died in 1851, and I paid off what was still owed. Thus, even his dying caused me expense. When my father died, my mother was left to me. She was by then in a strange state of mind from senile decay, and I assumed full financial responsibility for her as well. That same year, I signed a lease on Tavistock House, an eighteen-room stone mansion in London.

In 1853, I read publicly from my work before a large audience for the first time. It was a charitable undertaking to benefit the Industrial and Literary Institute in Birmingham. Three readings were scheduled. The first was on 27 December. Seventeen hundred people braved a snowstorm to attend. It is a good thing to have that many people together in the palm of one's hand. The final reading in the series was on 30 December. The audience was comprised of working people, who had been asked to pay only six pence apiece. I read to them from *A Christmas Carol*, not just as an author but as a stage performer, employing a different voice for each of the twenty-three characters.

Those in attendance listened closely with earnestness. Meeting with some of them after the reading, I saw a young woman with a cherubic face and golden hair and wondered if she might not be Florence Spriggs's daughter. Ruby would have been eighteen years old by then, the same age as this woman looked to be. But the young woman before me was from the north of England, and her parents were with her. The resemblance between mother and daughter was unmistakable.

Bleak House, Hard Times, Little Dorrit. My books grew in number.

I added a moustache and beard to my appearance. Friends said that they approved because they now saw less of me.

In 1858, I made the decision to read in public for my own financial profit. Some questioned the dignity of the undertaking and feared that it might damage my respectability. But there was no compromise of the literature.

I rehearsed the selection for each reading as many as a hundred times. Performances were in the evening, starting at eight o'clock. After ninety minutes, I would go to my dressing room for a ten-minute intermission, during which I had a glass of brandy or champagne. Then I returned to the stage for a final selection of about thirty minutes.

The readings were done from specially printed texts with large type and broad margins. In preparation, I deleted and reordered passages, marked each page with different coloured inks to denote stage instructions, and underlined phrases for emphasis.

My first reading for profit was conducted on 29 April at Saint Martin's Hall in London. I began by telling my audience, "I have long held the opinion that whatever brings a public man and his public face to face on terms of mutual confidence and respect is a good thing. Thus, it is that I come to be among you tonight, to hold with persons who would otherwise never hear my voice or see my face."

I read for three months in London and for three months more in other parts of England, Scotland, and Ireland. The crowds I saw every night welcomed me with affection and treated me as a friend.

But the happiness I had anticipated when I was young was not the happiness that I enjoyed. A vague longing shadowed me like a cloud. Years of marriage had provided me with little in the way of romance or companionship. I was a mismarried man.

Most men are disappointed in life somehow or

another. But a sense often came upon me of the most important friend that I had never made. Catherine was a kindhearted woman. But we were ill suited for one another, and there was no help for it.

There is no disparity in marriage more troublesome than unsuitability of mind. When I was young, I had made a terrible mistake. If Catherine had married another sort, she might have done better. As it was, we were poorly matched and bound together by a manacle forged of misfortune that joined our fettered hands so harshly that it chafed to the bone.

My affections for Catherine diminished steadily over time. Her presence aggravated me. As I grew leaner, she grew larger so that she was unpleasantly heavy. Plump became obese. Her face was very round. She fell into or out of every carriage we entered, scraped the skin off her legs, brought great sores on her feet, and made herself blue with bruises.

She was constantly pregnant, although I was as much to blame for that as she. Long after I lost feeling for her, we continued to have children. Catherine followed a pattern of pregnancy, birth, depression, and another pregnancy. As she aged, she suffered from violent headaches, melancholy, and nervous depression.

I became unbearably selfish, though I did not know it or refused to acknowledge that condition in myself. There was fault on my side in the intensity of my nature and the difficulties of my disposition. But nothing I might have done to better the situation would have altered the fact that the marriage was a weight upon me to which an anvil was a feather.

As Catherine and I grew more distant, I was given

to infatuations toward other women. She accused me often of infidelity. The accusations were false and infuriated me. I was unfaithful only in my heart. Other women crossed my path, but I acted beyond flirtation with none of them.

As the years passed, Amanda Wingate remained in my thoughts. She was a ghost that haunted me, an image of beauty stamped upon my heart, forever changeless and indelible. I preserved in my mind the image of her from each of the times we had met. The first day at her home; next, when I returned to interview Geoffrey Wingate for the second time; their dinner party; the ballet; and our assignation. The recollection of that late afternoon never dimmed in memory. There were periods in my life when I tried not to think of her. But always, she came back to me.

I have thought at times that no one can see Amanda with my eyes or know her with my mind. But then I wonder how many of my dreams have been dreamed by others and how many of those other dreamers were with her, as I was on that late afternoon in the spring.

I did not know what Amanda felt for me then nor what her remembrances were. Many times, I looked back upon that hour. Many times in the twilight of a summer evening or beside a flickering winter fire, my mind journeyed back to those moments. I dismissed Amanda from any association with my present or future as completely as if she were dead, which she might have been for all I knew. But she remained indelible in my thoughts like a great tower on a plain. In the innermost recesses of my mind, I cherished her against reason, against happiness, against peace.

I was at a loss to penetrate the mystery of my own heart. I never spoke to a soul about her. Over time, she became for me like a character of my creation whom I had loved and parted from forever when the writing of a book was done. She stood midway between the world of real people who populated my daily life and the fantasies of my mind.

My writing continued to be the only truly satisfying love of my life. I do not know why this was so. I know only that it was and remains true to this day.

I live in my books. Things do not exist for me until I have written them. The children of my mind, created and shaped as I wish them to be, are as real and as important to me as my flesh and blood children. They are my true progeny. Each time I finish the writing of a book, I bid farewell to family and friends who are dear to my heart. I am melancholy to think that they are lost to me forever and I will never see them again. I am happy and content only when I am writing. My cares lift when I sit with paper before me and pen in hand. If I stop writing, I will die.

It has been said often that I carry myself as though I am always on the stage. The passion that I had for theatre when I was young has been constant throughout my life. In the year after I was married, I wrote four plays. They were ordinary, and I acknowledged to myself that my literary gifts lay elsewhere. Thereafter, I acted in amateur theatrical productions and founded a theatrical company.

In 1857, I produced a play called *The Frozen Deep* at the Free Trade Hall in Manchester. Most of the actors and actresses in the cast were amateurs. But I engaged the services of three professionals: Frances Ternan and two of her daughters, Maria and Ellen.

Queen Victoria had ascended to the throne twenty years before. The Victorian era was characterised by a new moral restraint. Ladies of the aristocracy did not work in any occupation or engage in any other activity for pay. It was understood that some women were forced by circumstances to work. But acting—the display of a woman's body to men who paid for the pleasure of looking at her—was considered in some circles to be only one step removed from prostitution.

Ellen Ternan was graceful, witty, and charming—the antithesis of Catherine. I was forty-five years old when we met. "Nelly" was eighteen.

The passage of time had made it ever more difficult for Catherine and I to live together. My marriage had become a cold, bitter, taunting truth that bound me down as if with leaden chains. No two people were ever created with such an impossibility of interest, sympathy, or tenderness between them. Domestic unhappiness lay so heavily upon me that, for the first time in my life, it was difficult for me to write. Our marriage was no longer a matter of trial or will or sufferance or making the best of it. It was a blighted dismal failure that had to end.

In October of 1857, I instructed that the master bedroom and adjacent dressing room at Tavistock House be divided by a partition into separate bedrooms for Catherine and myself. But there was need to put a wider distance between us than could be found under one roof.

In May of 1858, negotiations for a marital separation began. In the end, an agreement was reached. Catherine left the marital residence and made a new home at 70 Gloucester Crescent. I agreed to pay the sum of six hundred pounds annually to her for the duration of her life. Our oldest son chose to live with his mother. The others, in accord with the deed of separation that Catherine and I signed, were given no choice and remained with me. Catherine's sister, Georgina, took my side and stayed at Tavistock to help look after the children and the running of the house.

I have been guilty on occasion of self-righteous behaviour. When things go wrong, I am inclined to portray myself as the sufferer and victim of others. I acknowledge that there were times when I conducted myself poorly during my marriage to Catherine. Too often, my passion was only for myself. I was cruel in ways that I should not have been. How much of my ungracious condition of mind was my own fault and how much of it was hers is of no moment now to me or to anyone else. Excusably or inexcusably, well or poorly done, the marriage was ended.

After Catherine and I separated, I was a friend to Ellen Ternan, her mother, and her sisters. I also developed a more personal attachment to Nelly. She was both purity and forbidden fruit.

A proper single woman did not have relations in bed with anyone, including the man she was engaged to marry. To do so would brand her as little more than a whore in the convention of the time. Nelly did not bend to my will as I had hoped she would. I kept after her and, by force of will, wore down her resistance. Finally, we had relations at my urging. But my attentions were a burden upon her. In the end, she told me, "It is over. It never should have begun."

Through it all, my fame continued to grow. The invention of the daguerreotype enabled the mass reproduction of images. By the late 1850s, the appearance of my photograph in newspapers and monthly publications was common, and my face was known throughout England. At times, I felt as though my visage had been sufficiently printed and distributed to haunt mankind forever.

My public readings continued. I advanced in fame and fortune to the approving roar of the crowd. I was the only author that many among England's deprived classes knew.

I also became a property owner. When I was a boy, my father brought me often to look at a house called Gad's Hill Place. "Do you see that house?" he told me. "If you grow up to be a wealthy man, perhaps you shall own that house or another like it."

The Gad's Hill property was put up for sale. I paid the purchase price. The leasee's term expired. In September of 1860, I moved in.

My intense activity continued.

A Tale of Two Cities . . . *Great Expectations* . . . *Our Mutual Friend*.

I rarely relaxed. I was never fully at rest. I was always dissatisfied and trying after something that I was never able to find.

The seasons passed. More years went by. A field of flowers bloomed by a river that flowed sparkling in the summer sun. Then snow covered the field and the river rolled to the sea, ruffled by the winter wind and thickened with drifting ice.

I grew older. My health began to fail. I suffered at times from prolonged colds, sore throats, congestion of the chest, and weariness that lasted for weeks. There were days when my left foot was so swollen from gout that I could not put on my boot. On some nights, I relied upon opium to sleep.

On the ninth day of November in 1867, I set sail from London for a second American tour. Twenty-five years earlier, I had visited America to see the country and its people and gather notes for a book. The motivation for this trip was profit alone. Eighty-four readings were planned for a guarantee of ten thousand pounds with the likelihood of earning twice as much.

I arrived in Boston on the nineteenth of November. Within a day, every ticket for my readings there had been sold. I travelled next to New York, where it seemed as though my bust or portrait was in every shop I entered. In Washington, President Andrew Johnson reserved seats for each performance for his family and himself. A quarter century earlier, President Tyler had greeted me with the encomium, "I am astonished to see so young a man, sir." Now there were whispers that I looked old.

For much of the tour, I suffered from a cold. My gout flared, and my left foot was painfully swollen. Because of my condition, readings in Chicago and Canada were cancelled.

The journey closed with a return to Boston followed by five farewell readings in New York. My last appearance was on the twentieth of April, 1868. I rose, as was my custom, at seven in the morning and had fresh cream with two tablespoons of rum. At noon, I partook of a sherry cobbler and a biscuit. Then I visited the hall to review the surroundings one last time.

A maroon carpet had been placed on the stage with a large maroon screen as a backdrop. Gaslights were aligned in a manner that would present me in the most dramatic light possible while the rest of the stage receded into darkness. A reading desk stood at the center of the stage, covered by a crimson cloth. Late in the day, I put on my evening clothes, affixed a boutonniere to the satin lapel on my tailcoat, and ate an egg mixed into a glass of sherry.

The reading began at eight o'clock. I was greeted by enthusiastic applause. I felt well. My energy was uncharacteristically strong. I read from *The Pickwick Papers* and *A Christmas Carol*, gesturing with both hands, grimacing, glaring, and rolling my eyes as I performed. At the end, I addressed the crowd.

"In this brief life of ours, it is sad to do almost anything for the last time. It is a sad consideration with me that, in a very few moments, this brilliant hall and all that it contains will fade from my view for evermore. When I first entered on this interpretation of myself, I was sustained by the hope that I could drop into some hearts some new expression of the meaning of my books. To this hour, that purpose is strong. In all probability, I shall never see your faces again. But I can assure you that yours have yielded me as much pleasure as I have given to you."

There was thunderous applause. As a matter of course, I usually left the stage at that moment, went to my dressing room, and did not return. But on this, my last night in America, I lingered.

The applause grew louder. I stepped down the stairs into the space between the stage and the front row to mingle with the crowd. People were pushing their way down the aisle, shouting my name, struggling to come close to me within the mob. There was chaos.

Then I saw an apparition.

I stood transfixed.

My face grew flush.

The apparition came closer.

All time seemed suspended.

And the apparition spoke.

"You've done quite well for yourself, Mr. Dickens," Amanda Wingate said.

CHAPTER 11

She was changed, of course. Time had set some marks
upon her face. Her fine figure was a shade less upright
than when I had known her, and her hair was gray. But
the passing years had given her their blessing. If her
beauty was no longer in the spring of life, it was certainly not in winter. There was a contentment in her
eyes that I had not seen before.

The woman I had longed for my entire life was
standing in front of me. In that moment, I would have
died for her.

"You were always beautiful. But you are more beautiful now than ever."

"Father Time does his work honestly," Amanda said
with a smile. "I do not mind him."

The crowd was pushing in around us.

"May I take you to dinner tonight?"

"Thank you, but that is not possible."

"I must see you again."

"I simply wanted to tell you that I am happy for your success and wish you well."

A stout red-faced man inserted himself between us and clamped his hand on mine. The smell of onions was heavy on his breath. He resembled a slobbering, overfed cow.

"Mr. Dickens. It is an honour and a pleasure—"

I cut him off.

"And I say to you, Mr. Dickens, to have you in our city and to shake your hand—"

More people were closing in. I struggled to free myself from his grip.

"The hand that has written so many fine books, the hand—"

I broke free. Amanda was gone. I searched frantically for her with my eyes, but she had disappeared into the crowd. I tried to move to where she might be and was swallowed up by the mob.

An hour later, I returned to the hotel. I was wet with sweat. My heart was pounding. My emotions were in turmoil. The concierge called my name.

"Mr. Dickens, a package for you."

I accepted a box wrapped in paper the colour of gold.

"When did this come?"

"Early in the evening."

"By whose hand?"

"A woman, sir. She did not leave her name."

"What did she look like?"

"Not a young woman, sir. But extremely attractive and nicely dressed. There was an elegance about her."

I took the package hurriedly to my room, tore off the paper . . . and held a book in my hands. Exquisitely

and freshly bound in soft brown leather with marbled
end boards and gold letters on the cover: *Sketches by Boz,
Volume I.*

I turned to the title page and, beneath the title, read:

> *For Amanda Wingate,*
> *a woman of uncommon beauty and grace.*
> *My fondest good wishes,*
> *Charles Dickens*

She had kept it. All these years, down every road she
had travelled, I had travelled with her.

A letter sealed with red wax lay nestled between the
pages. The stationery was the colour of cream, edged
in cobalt blue:

> *Dear Mr. Dickens,*
>
> *For many years, I have read your books with happiness for
> your success. It is an extraordinary world, and I have followed
> your passage through it with great joy. I know of your life
> through the newspapers and reading your books. Let me tell you
> of my own years.*
>
> *Long ago when we knew each other, I was in chains.
> I loathed my life but had gone too far to turn back. I was
> obligated under the law and in the eyes of God to fulfill my
> marriage vows. Geoffrey was a broken man when we left
> England. The fear of punishment that was instilled in him
> caused the wounds of which he died. His life ended by his own
> hand.*
>
> *I am happy now. I have been married for many years to a
> good man. He knows of my past and accepts it. We met after
> the death of his wife and, together, raised his son and daughter.*

We have grandchildren now. I have held them in my arms since they were born. I am at peace with myself and who I am.

I have thought often of you. I remember our time together with great fondness. You were a better friend to me than I was accustomed to having at that time in my life. You have been a better companion to me these many years than you could possibly have known. We will continue to be friends though we are apart.

I hope that your happiness has rivaled your fame and continues to do so.

Warmest regards,
Amanda

I wept.

Uncontrollably.

Loss and grief swept over me.

Amanda had found in the arms of another man what I have never known. I had longed for her, and only her, for more than thirty years. I was infinitely sad and broken.

I slept not at all that night. I am Dickens, renowned throughout England as the greatest wordsmith since Shakespeare. Yet my words had failed me. I had been constricted in the lecture hall by the throng that surrounded us. She had appeared when I could not speak my heart. Yet I should have fallen to my knees and paid the crowd no mind. And if I had . . . it would have been to no avail.

There was no way to find her. Her letter was signed simply "Amanda."

I looked at myself in the mirror. A haggard face confronted me. I examined the lines and hollows. I felt useless and older than my fifty-six years.

Life is made up of partings. This one caused me to suffer the most. I returned home to England, safe but not sound. The last remnants of my heart were shattered.

⸙

Two years have passed since that time. I have conducted public readings when my health allows. The last was at Saint James Hall in London on 15 March of this year. Except for this writing, I believe that my most important work is done.

I think often of Amanda. I cannot help it. I live with what might have been and what was not. For four and thirty years, I have been haunted by the memory of her. And I have treasured it. Had that late afternoon between us not happened, would my life be emptier or more serene? Are there strings in the human heart that are best not vibrated? Did she perhaps feel some love for me? There are so many unanswered questions.

I do not know. I do not know.

I know only that I loved her and heaped upon her the wealth of my imagination. It is no better or worse because I write of it. Nothing can make it other than as it was. My dreams of Amanda live now only at night and melt away in the first beam of sunlight, leaving me sadder than when I lay down the night before. I would forsake everything in my life for her. But the ocean is between us, and I am resigned to think of her as if she were beneath another sun and sky.

The future is a bright thought for some, wreathed with cheerful hopes. The time for me, when the thought of love would have been filled with optimism, is gone. The Creator bestows youth but once and never grants it again. I have outlived the dreams that I once cherished. My course is nearly run.

There is a large grandfather clock in the dining room of my home. Its face is brass and silver with just a touch of gold. The steady pendulum throbs and beats in the bottom of the old dark case. The pulse of the craftsman who made it was stilled long ago.

How often in the tranquility of night, when the clock and I are the only things in the house that are awake, have its chimes broken the silence and given me assurance that it watches faithfully over me. How often have I marvelled at its constancy, its freedom from human strife and desire, its steadiness of purpose, and its ceaseless going on. It is the voice of time, reminding me that my brief sojourn on earth will soon be lost in a vast eternity as a drop of water is lost in the sea.

My health is poor. Words come slowly to me now, in speech and as I write. My eyesight is weak. I am dizzy from time to time. My left leg does not always do what my mind commands it to do. My left hand some times misses the mark when performing a simple chore.

As I write these words, the blaze is departing from the fireplace in my study. The afterglow will soon subside. The ashes will turn gray and drop to dust. I am about to pass through change of a similar kind. More often now, my thoughts of London wander to the river which flows through the city and rolls steadily away to meet the sea. I am on the brink of that great gulf that no one can see beyond. Some day soon, my bed will be a coffin in which I lie in calm and lasting sleep, with tall grass waving gently above my head and the sound of church bells to soothe me.

I believe that I am a good man. I ask forgiveness from all whom I have wronged. Whatever I have done in life, I have tried with all my heart to do well. I have never put my hand to anything on which I could not throw my whole self thoroughly and in earnest. I have devoted myself completely to aims great and small.

My greatest happiness has been in my written words. There have been few times when I was truly happy except in my books. My purpose in life is writing. I measure myself by my art. My books will speak for me when my faults and virtues, my fortunes and misfortunes, are all long forgotten.

My great ambition has been to live in the hearts and homes of the English people through the truthful telling of English life. In my writing, future generations will find London and the English people as they have been in my time. I have tried without cessation to give common men and women a voice so that they may be heard and to use my fame and talent to combat the sordid oppression of their daily lives.

Every effort of my pen has been intended to elevate the poor and downtrodden to the station they deserve. I have always endeavoured to present them in as favourable a light as the rich and to advocate their being made as happy as the circumstances of their condition in its utmost improvement will allow. I will fight to my last breath the dreadful engines of a society which makes young children old before they know what childhood is and gives them the exhaustion and infirmities of old age without the privilege of old age to die. I have tried to make a difference. My God, I have tried.

To leave one's hand lastingly upon time in a way that time itself cannot obliterate is to lift oneself above the dust of Kings in their graves. I hope that, centuries from now, people will read my books and, through them, know me and the age in which I lived. A hundred years from now, which will be more real? The lives of David Copperfield and Oliver Twist, or the lives of the millions upon millions of people who are alive today but will be gone and forgotten soon after their last breath?

My mind wanders often now to the eternal tread of feet upon the streets of London. The hand that traces these words falters as it approaches the completion of its task. This baring of private emotions has been difficult for me. But I have fulfilled the vow that I made to myself to reflect my mind honestly and fully and to bring my secrets to light.

When I think of Amanda, the past comes out of its grave. Decades vanish, and I am in a time of my life when the qualities that have done me the most good were growing in my heart. The whole world lay before me, bathed in the light of hope and youth. By this writing, my passion for Amanda shall outlive me. Our names will be forever joined.

Amanda was born into a world where generation upon generation of good men and women rise each day, lie down each night, live and die, with no certain roof over their head but the lid of a coffin to shelter them some day. They awake each morning not knowing where their head will rest that night. They seek not a luxurious life, but the bare means of subsistence to continue their struggle for another day. Many among them die in spirit when they are young. They know only injustice and misery. Knowledge is never taught. Yet the world rolls on, careless and indifferent to their plight.

Amanda did more than survive that world. She over-came the squalor of her origins. She found happiness. She triumphed!

Now, as I close this writing, many faces fade away. But one face shines before me like a radiant Heavenly light. It is the face of a lady. She is very beautiful. And I love her.

Charles Dickens
Gad's Hill Place
30 May 1870

Note to the Reader

On the night of 8 June 1870, while dining at home, Charles Dickens suffered a massive cerebral hemorrhage. He lapsed into unconsciousness and never moved or spoke again. Death came the following afternoon several hours before sunset. He was buried in Westminster Abbey. For two days, tens of thousands of people, most of them common men and women, passed by his open grave to pay their respects and drop flowers onto his coffin.

Shortly after Dickens's death, a locked box was found among his belongings with a letter directing that the box be transferred to the British Museum and kept unopened in a library vault until the two hundredth anniversary of his birth.

The box was opened in private on 7 February 2012. In it, those present at the opening found a leather-bound copy of *Sketches by Boz, Volume I*, the foregoing manuscript, and a silk handkerchief with two violets embroidered into the cloth.

In accord with what are believed to have been Mr. Dickens's wishes, the manuscript is published herewith.

About the Author

New York Times bestselling author Thomas Hauser was born in New York and attended both college and law school at Columbia University. After graduating from law school, he clerked for a federal judge. Then he started work as a litigator for the Wall Street law firm of Cravath Swaine & Moore.

In 1977, Hauser began to write. Since then, he has authored forty-seven books, on subjects ranging from professional boxing to Beethoven. He has been published by many of the major imprints in the US and UK publishing industries, including Simon & Schuster, Viking Penguin, Collins, Touchstone, Warner Books, Pan Macmillan, and Hamish Hamilton.

His first book, *Missing,* was nominated for the Pulitzer Prize, the Bancroft Prize, and the National Book Award and was the basis for the Academy Award–winning film starring Jack Lemmon and Sissy Spacek. *The Beethoven Conspiracy,* Hauser's thriller about the search for a lost Beethoven symphony, won the prestigious Prix Lafayette, awarded biannually in France to the outstanding book by an American. Subsequently, Hauser co-authored *Final Warning: The Legacy of Chernobyl,* again demonstrating his ability to bring to life and explain events of complexity and importance, an ability that has secured his reputation as a responsible and reliable social critic. The film version of *Final Warning* starred Jon Voight and Jason Robards.

Hauser's most celebrated work to date is *Muhammad Ali: His Life and Times*—the definitive biography of the man who was once the most famous person on earth. Like *Missing,* the Ali book was nominated for a Pulitzer Prize and the National Book Award. The British edition was honored with the William Hill Sports Book of the Year Award in England. Subsequently, Ali and Hauser coauthored *Healing: A Journal of Tolerance and Understanding,* and they crisscrossed the country, meeting with student audiences on their subject. For their efforts to combat bigotry and prejudice, they were named as co-recipients of the 1998 Haviva Reik Peace Award.

In recent years, Hauser has written extensively about the sport and business of professional boxing. His award-winning investigative articles and his testimony before the United States Senate Committee on Commerce, Science, and Transportation were hailed within the boxing industry as a significant force for change.

In 2004, he was honored by the Boxing Writers Association of America, which bestowed on him the Nat Fleischer Award for Career Excellence in Boxing Journalism.

Hauser's books are read worldwide in eighteen languages. He has published articles in *The New Yorker*, *The New York Times*, and numerous other publications, and he was retained by the *Encyclopedia Britannica* to write its entries on Muhammad Ali and Arnold Palmer. He is currently a consultant to HBO Sports and has appeared in several HBO documentaries in addition to being featured in the Academy Award–winning documentary *When We Were Kings* and being interviewed on numerous television programs such as NBC's *The Today Show*.

He lives in Manhattan.

Printed in the United States
by Baker & Taylor Publisher Services